Return Passage

RETURN PASSAGE

Michael Harvey

Copyright © Michael Harvey 1991

ISBN 1-878555-02-2

Oakbridge University Press
6716 Eastside Drive N.E., Suite 50
Tacoma, Washington 98422

Cover photo by Lee McClellan

For Shirley

CHAPTER 1

Death, Where is thy Sting?

The screaming, shuddering, roaring sounds of battle swept over me: machine guns chattering their voices of death, splinters of shrapnel screeching into the distance, yells of command becoming indistinguishable as shades of darkness descended like a shroud. Sergeant Richard Nelson, Calgary Highlanders, Second Division, Canadian Army... killed in action prior to his twentieth birthday while advancing through the cold, flooded plain of the Scheldt Estuary in Belgium.

I was Richard Nelson.

This is my story.

Return Passage

The 6th German Paratroop Regiment was well dug in on the dikes of Woensdrecht.... We huddled miserably in shallow, water-filled slit trenches, our meager shelter in the flat fields the Germans had flooded by breaching the dike. At 0630 hours the thunder of our artillery heralded the attack. Leaving our trenches, we followed a creeping barrage, stopping only when we were within twenty-five yards of the bursting shells, pausing until the firing ceased, then churning forward through the mud toward the German positions.

The heavy anti-aircraft shells from our 3.7 inch guns were timed to burst just above the paratroopers' position. This, we hoped, would keep their heads down long enough for us to climb the steep sides of the dike to overrun their positions. We had underestimated the tenacity of the Germans. For as soon as the firing ceased, they opened up with every weapon they had, including lethal 88's, to rain a murderous wall of fire into our ranks. The casualties were staggering.

Suddenly the earth heaved, an irresistible force throwing me to the blood-spattered ground. I didn't realize what had happened. I seemed to float as if I were suspended by some giant balloon. I could still see the platoon advancing as before. Nicholson was firing short bursts from his Bren gun as his section provided the "leg on the ground." The other sections, firing as they moved, were scrambling forward as quickly as the mud would allow. I could hear the rattle of machine guns, the crashing of high explosives, the moan of shrapnel.

Clearly I could see Lieutenant Sharp, young and inexperienced, calling on his radio for additional artillery support. I wondered how long he'd last; we'd averaged a new platoon officer about every three weeks. I felt as if I were in a nightmare from which I couldn't awaken. I was needed by the platoon with whom I'd fought since shortly after D-Day.

I must be hallucinating, I thought. Although I felt as alive as ever, I could now see myself lying grotesquely lifeless, entrails oozing from my belly into the mud of the Scheldt.

Return Passage

I was bewildered more than frightened. I tried to rationalize. Perhaps I was dying while my brain, deprived of blood, played tricks on me. Maybe the Medic had given me morphine.... Then I seemed to hear the soft voice of a woman calling from afar, urging me to follow the light. I turned my eyes away from the battle to the sound of the voice. Instead of a person I viewed a golden light swirling like a vortex in the graying sky. From within the swirling light, more distinctly now, was a sweet voice urging me forward.

I seemed to float toward the vortex, moving faster and faster. Swiftly, I was totally engulfed in a spiraling tunnel that flung me forward in a roaring fury of sound. The staccato sounds of battle faded, my forward momentum slowed, brilliant colors swam before my eyes. Then stillness, like that of a forest glade, muted all sound. Colors coming into brilliant focus, a landscape of indescribable beauty. A small group of people moving toward me. I immediately recognized one of them... Sonia.

CHAPTER 2

Reunion

I should have remembered, of course, as there had been many such transformations over the centuries as my spirit found freedom from bodily functions. The truth rushes back as the deceits and lies of the slower vibration fade. I'm again in that realm of understanding: that spiritual oasis of refurbishment, rest and determination that will provide the strength for my next journey, the journey that will eventually lead to my becoming one again with my Creator.

My body now decays in death not far from where my previous body was buried in 1918. Neither is missed. There had not been great opportunity to advance spiritually in my life as Richard Nelson. Nor had there been any great setback to prior progress I'd made in other lifetimes. Due to war, both lifetimes were very short. I would soon learn, again, the misery I had endured in these lives was created not by others, as I'd thought, but by myself.

I was sure I was hallucinating as Sonia and the group approached. The one person I'd loved, in the mystical, intoxicating, soul-searing first love of youth, had been Sonia, a member of the Canadian Women's Army Corps. But Sonia had died in an accident. I'd attended her funeral and shed bitter tears in the silence of my inner being. Nevertheless, there she stood, a hint of gold in cascading hair reaching for her shoulders, her eyes reflecting the mischievous tenderness that seared my heart.

She took a pace forward from the others. "Hello, Rick, my darling." Whether I was crazy, hallucinating or having the final flickering thoughts of a dying brain didn't matter. I rushed forward to take her in my arms, fearful, that like the cobwebs of a dream, the vision would vanish. But it didn't as I crushed her against me.

Another of the group stepped forward to stand directly behind Sonia. "Tim Cowan, for God's sake," I laughed. "Now I know I'm crazy or dreaming. You were decapitated by a shell three weeks ago. That's when they promoted me platoon sergeant to take your place."

Tim grinned, placing his arm over Sonia's shoulder to rest his hand on mine. "You're not dreaming or crazy Richard. We're all real — me, Sonia, everybody. We've simply changed vibrations and entered a different reality."

"We sure as hell have." I returned Tim's grin as the entire episode was deliciously ridiculous, better than any dream I had ever experienced. Here I was holding the girl I loved and whom I knew, without doubt, was dead, talking to a comrade who had been killed before my eyes a matter of three weeks ago. In the back of my mind the probable realities of the situation again flickered a warning. It was the effect of morphine; perhaps even now I was being evacuated to a field hospital, if I were lucky. Or maybe these were the antics of a brain denying death.

I looked closely at Tim. Every feature was exactly as I remembered, even the little mole to the side of his left eye. His battle dress, I noted, was clean, no longer soaked in blood from the torn stump of his neck that no longer supported a head. "Tim, I think you're full of shit," I laughed. "You're dead. I know because I helped pick up the pieces...."

Sonia's arm tightened around me so that I looked again into those beautiful eyes. "I know it's difficult to grasp initially, darling. It was even more difficult for me to accept my bodily death in the truck crash. You see, people who really mattered to me in that life were still in bodily form — my parents and you, especially. Of course, I met many souls I had encountered in a previous existence, which helped. But now you have the advantage of meeting souls with whom you shared your most recent existence. War, I suppose, has some compensations when you arrive over here."

I still wasn't fully convinced that this was anything other than my mind playing tricks. "Okay, I'll take your word for it, Sonia and Tim. But if what you say is true — that we're all dead and in another vibration or reality — is this then what we called heaven or, maybe, hell, seeing that you are here, Tim?" The last remark was my way of making a joke about something I couldn't grasp. All I knew was that after the cold, bloodied-mud hell of the Scheldt, this seemed like heaven.

There were other people in the group. In single file they approached. There was no mistaking any of them. Leading was freckled-faced, red-complexioned Duncan Watson, looking exactly as he had looked at Southside Boys School. He squeezed my hand, which I reluctantly removed from Sonia's back. "Better get the old soccer strip on, Richard," he smiled. "They say that the team from Saint George's is out for revenge."

Duncan was referring to the fact we both played on the school soccer team and had soundly whipped the larger and more elite Saint George's team for the title back in the early 1940's. Everything transpiring was ludicrous. We were standing in an incredible countryside of breathtaking beauty, my arms held my dead girlfriend, I was in uniform and hadn't played soccer since 1942, my ex-platoon sergeant Tim Cowan, who had been decapitated, now stood listening to our conversation. . . and Duncan Watson had been drowned when he was about thirteen years of age.

The next to last person in the group stepped forward to take Duncan's place. I gave an involuntary gasp as I recognized the only female teacher at Southside, Mrs. Dunne. Mrs. Dunne had been the only ray of light to pierce the oppression of those long, tormented days at school. She taught my favorite subject — history — bringing it alive with vivid description.

In the latter days of her life she had suffered a dreadful illness. Some elders had whispered it would be a blessing if she passed away. I learned later it was cancer. My most distinct memory of her had been as a rather heavy-set, jolly woman with a Northern England accent. Her iron-gray hair was worn close to her head in a bun. Behind steel-rimmed glasses, eyes of light blue sparkled with the enthusiasm of instilling knowledge.

Sonia stepped to one side as Mrs. Dunne's large female figure bore down on us. She enfolded me against her ample bosom as time vanished and I again smelled lilac, the fragrance I always associated with her. "Little Richard Nelson," she breathed, "how wonderful to be with you again." I returned her hug. During all my days of misery at Southside she had been the only one to whom I could turn. The last time I had seen her was in a hospital room. She lay pathetic, thin and lifeless, looking almost like a little girl's plaster doll. She couldn't speak; I doubted she knew I had come to see her. She died early the next morning.

CHAPTER 3

A Major Revelation

The last of the group stepped forward. Involuntarily my arm arched up in salute, for it was Major MacDougal, the finest company commander in the regiment, an officer we all liked and respected. The major had "bought it" (as we called being killed in action) while leading us across a strongly defended German position. The Germans commanded the heights with a clear view and field of fire. Mortars, heavy machine guns and dug-in artillery poured a curtain of screaming steel across our line of advance.

One platoon, under Lieutenant Billings, had rushed the heights but had been thrown back with heavy casualties. Field artillery and tank support were called upon. The German-held ridge was blasted with a murderous barrage while the second platoon in the company moved up under the protective shield. Seconds after the barrage lifted, the Germans resumed firing. The fact that they survived the devastating high explosive was unbelievable. But the ground was sodden, lessening the effect of the shrapnel, and we were again opposed by the cream of the German Army, the disciplined, courageous 6th Paratroop Regiment. The second assault also ended in failure and heavy casualties.

After two abortive attempts to dislodge the enemy, it is often better to lick your wounds, regroup and plan an attack with stronger forces. Our Typhoons were grounded due to weather conditions. Tomorrow, if it cleared, we could hit the Germans from the air. Major MacDougal, we were informed, had received new orders from battalion headquarters. "Attack again," was the curt command. "It is vital for the entire division that this enemy-held ridge be captured before nightfall."

Some company commanders would simply launch another attack from the comparative safety of their command post. Not MacDougal. He knew morale was low. He knew what must be done. The support fire again roared over our heads as Major MacDougal led the attack up the ridge. He was like a man possessed, yelling, urging us on, oblivious to the deadly fire hurled toward us.

Leading the attack, firing from the hip, the Major spearheaded our charge into the German positions. Support Company's three-inch mortars spat a continuous rain of high explosives on the German position. The platoon's own two-inch mortars lobbed smoke bombs to hamper the defenders. Vickers machine guns sputtered on the flanks, throwing continuing short bursts into the enemy lines. Sweating, swearing, screaming, we scrambled behind our Major toward the German positions.

Major MacDougal was first on the ridge. I saw him gain the top, firing as he broached the German trench. Single-handed, he destroyed a heavy machine gun crew and the infantrymen who came to their aid. We poured over the German positions, blasting and bayoneting. They fought back courageously, firing from their bunkers until silenced by death. As the ridge was now ours, we turned to our commander, expecting him to prepare for a counter attack. He sat with his back to the trench wall as if exhausted. Then we saw the small dark hole just above his left eye and that the back of his skull was missing.

But now the Major stood as he had in life: tall, heavy-set, ruddy complexioned, his bushy mustache topping a half smile. His blue eyes bore into mine as if he were expecting me to acknowledge his presence. "I still think my mind is playing tricks on me, Sir," I stammered, "but if you give me the word I'll do my best to adapt."

Major MacDougal smiled broadly, waved a casual salute and with the hint of a laugh ordered, "Carry on, Sergeant."

I turned again to Sonia, gently tipping her face so that I could gaze directly into her eyes. "If it is true we are all dead, then surely God must be here; is He? And is this place the Heaven the Bible mentions?" She squeezed me tightly before replying, "Most of us here are relative newcomers. The only exceptions are your school friends, Mrs. Dunne and Duncan Watson. That means that the remainder of us are only scratching the surface of understanding. You'll learn soon enough that this place is our real home, more so than any of the temporary abodes we've had on earth. The lives we lead in the slower vibrations of bodily form are the dream, the half-illusionary unreality. You'll find out, Richard, that this is a place of love, learning and understanding."

Sonia paused to wave to the group of friends, who began drifting away. "You see, darling, we've lived here countless times before setting out on our numerous earthbound journeys. Although each lifetime seemed to take years in flesh form, it was just a blink of an eyelid in eternity. All human beings are really spiritual creatures, therefore eternal. There is no such thing as death...."

She smiled, snuggling close, smiling happily. My bewilderment must have been evident, for she continued. "I realize it's pretty hard to grasp at first, particularly when your body has been killed violently. I can remember my trauma as I realized my body was dead after the truck accident. But no matter how we leave the bodily vibration, old and feeble, a heart attack, an accident or some horrible illness, our earthly body is just like a uniform or suit of clothes. When it has served its purpose, it is discarded. When our guides and we determine we're ready for a new earthbound journey, we emerge in a new body as a baby. It's like going to the Quartermaster's for a new uniform.

"But, come now", she said, grasping my hand. "You've had enough excitement for one day. Tomorrow you'll have beings far more knowledgeable than I explaining things to you. I have only one further thing to say now. This is neither heaven nor hell. It's a way station, so to speak, on the journey to become one with our

Creator. God, of course, is here within us, as God is within everything. It is the same way on the earth plane, by the way. Hell is symbolic for being screened from God, a condition where the shadow of ignorance blocks out the light of the Creator's love."

I don't remember much more of that experience. All I vaguely recall is being led by Sonia into a beautiful room. Then, without undressing, lying on a deliciously soft bed after she'd pulled a luxurious eiderdown over us, I felt the warmth of her body pressing close to mine as I drifted into a deep, refreshing sleep.

CHAPTER 4

Loving Explanations

A golden radiance filled the room to herald the beginning of my first full day in the place Sonia had described as a way station. While refreshed and well, I was still confused about my surroundings and status. My body was as solid as it had ever been. Strangely, there was no sign whatsoever of that massive wound I'd received.

Once I'd heard that a drowning person sees his lifetime pass before his eyes. Nothing like that had happened to me. There'd only been that vortex of light and sound that had seemed to transport me to my happy reunion with Sonia and the others.

The thought of Sonia raised a tremor of panic. Where was she? "Sonia," I called, fearing all events were an illusion. "Darling, you're awake." I heard her reply as she burst through the open door and threw herself on the bed and into my outstretched arms. This was no illusion. This was a replay of a love that had been torn from me by death. I didn't stop to think that our passionate embraces hadn't led to sex as it would have when on earth. Here fulfillment was reached in an energy exchange in which we seemed to merge into one. Strangely, this experience was more gratifying than anything ever experienced. When the electrifying excitement of passion gave way to a deep, satisfying feeling of overwhelming love, I began to ask the multitude of questions that sprang to mind. Sonia laughed softly before replying that she, as she had explained to me yesterday, was a relative newcomer in the way station and souls far more knowledgeable than she would give me all the answers.

Her use of the word "souls" puzzled me. "Are we not people — you, me, and all the others I met yesterday?" I wanted to know. "Because if we aren't, I've never seen such realistic flesh and blood people. And, if you're not a real person," I laughed, patting her bum, "then I'm a ghost in a white sheet."

Her eyelids crinkled in a characteristic way that indicated she was suppressing laughter. "I think I can explain this because it is the question that puzzled me when I first arrived. They tell me...." I asked who she meant by "they."

"The guides, Richard. You'll find out about them soon enough. They say that all beings, whether we're here or in bodily form on earth, are souls that are merely clothed in bodies of flesh and blood for our adventures of learning.

"Actually, that isn't true here," she giggled before continuing. "Here it is more like bodies of the imagination. When the earthly body dies, the pure essence of the soul departs. But a soul is a spirit being. It doesn't occupy space. It can't be captured. It is pure energy." I was puzzled as this was pretty heady stuff, especially on the first morning of a new existence. Sonia brushed her lips against my cheek and continued. "Do you remember when we had that long weekend together and I told you that I wanted to write a poem so that I would always remember the love we shared?"

I nodded, for that little interlude had angered me. That she should waste nearly an hour sitting at a desk writing on hotel notepaper when we had so little time together was, I thought, silly. After Sonia's death that poem had become my most valuable possession. Read and reread. A link to a most wonderful memory. I still carried it in the inner pocket of my battle dress tunic.

"Well, you will remember that I didn't write continuously. Sometimes I just sat there, apparently staring into space. Don't you remember accusing me of that?" I nodded guiltily, urging her to continue. "What do you think I was doing when I sat doing nothing?" I answered she had been thinking of the way to best rhyme those deep inner feelings she was trying to convey.

"You're right, sweetheart," she smiled. "That is exactly what I was doing, thinking of our love and trying to express it in simple words. Now the point is this: you couldn't see the thoughts in my head, could you?"

I nodded my agreement, wondering what point she was trying to make. "Well then, the question is: were my thoughts realities? Did they exist and were they concrete facts? You'll have to agree they were, indeed, as they came to fruition in the poem."

I still felt bewildered though I had listened to her explanation with great intensity. I admitted, sheepishly, I was now so baffled I'd forgotten the question I'd asked. She dazzled a smile in my direction. "You didn't ask a direct question. You just looked so puzzled when I explained that a soul is a spirit of pure energy. I thought that my little story about the poem would enable you to see the reality of spiritual existence."

I still wasn't sure I understood, but Sonia told me that the guides would explain everything. Meanwhile, being with Sonia was good enough for me.

CHAPTER 5

Samantha

Sonia had said more advanced souls would take over my education. I wasn't the least bit prepared for the individuals who presented themselves to carry out the job, despite Sonia's assurance that my personal guide would become the most important person in my life.

The guides turned out to be the two most striking individuals I'd ever encountered. Sonia's was male, spectacularly tall, and resembled a contemporary painting of Christ. His hair curled softly to his shoulders. Deep, dark eyes displayed a compassionate intelligence arousing a feeling of reverence. His deep, melodious voice sounded like the lower notes of a pipe organ.

The woman who would be my personal guide was equally enchanting. She had silver-colored hair cascading over her head and shoulders, reflecting sunlight like prisms made by the spray of a waterfall. Her eyes reflected the glory of an innate gentleness. Her voice, like her companion's, was low and melodious... more like a song than normal speech. Her age I couldn't guess, but not a blemish marred her magnificent features. She was, without a doubt, the most beautiful person I had seen.

She looked at me directly, unblinkingly, then smiled. "I'm Samantha, Richard. I am your companion and guide just as John is Sonia's. You and I will be spending much time together, as we have in the past." I was both delighted and bewildered: enthralled that I would be spending my time with so gorgeous a creature, confused as, to my knowledge, I had never before laid eyes upon her.

(I reflected that John and Sonia being together aroused not the slightest tinge of jealousy. I somehow felt that the relationship was unlike anything previously experienced. The same feelings were evident in Sonia. In earthly life her eyes had blazed angrily when she thought another woman was encroaching on her territory; now she merely accepted Samantha's presence with tranquility.)

We sat on chairs I hadn't noticed before, Sonia facing John and Samantha facing me. I remarked about my lack of observation to Samantha, who, smiling, responded, "You'll find that necessity has the power to produce whatever is needed in this environment, Richard. You must be comfortable, as the time has come to undergo the experiences you missed after the death of your body."

This was frightening until she placed a hand of velvet over mine, leaned closer, absorbing me with her gentle, knowing eyes, and said, "You mustn't be afraid; this is just the start of many lessons to help you to advance spiritually.

"These experiences are never any better or any worse than they were at the time they happened. They are merely your experiences, with the added dimension of feeling the happiness, love or hurt and loneliness you produced in others. It is just a matter of growing spiritually through the realization of what our lifetime has meant to those with whom we have come in contact."

Samantha told me that we would be joined by a spirit Being of high order whose presence would be felt but who would not be visible. I was not yet ready to view the reality of the dimension I now inhabited, she said. That would come later. I asked how the viewing of my past life would take place and what was I to do? "Do nothing, Richard," she replied. "Simply take a couple of deep breaths, close your eyes and listen."

Return Passage

I obeyed her suggestion, making myself as comfortable as possible while listening to the soft melody of her voice describing an imaginary journey to a beautiful sea shore. She was a masterful storyteller for soon I could vividly see everything she described in my imagination. I lay on a beach with the hot sun blazing, cooled by gentle breezes drifting through the palm trees ringing a lagoon. The waves gently lapped over the sands; I felt heavy and warm, my eyelids felt like lead shields; I was drifting away into sleep.

CHAPTER 6

Misery Relived

I'm really not sure if it were a proper sleep or a trance. Soon Samantha's voice became only a murmur in the distance as startlingly clear pictures began to form in my mind. I could see myself as a little boy in the distance. I drew closer to the scene until it engulfed me. For now I had become the image. I was again the child who had been me.

My mother was speaking with an exasperated tone. "Richard, don't be silly. Lots of little boys go to boarding school if their parents can afford it. You are six years of age, not a baby, and you have to face things like a little soldier." I tried to swallow the large lump constricting my throat, merely increasing the flow of tears.

Life was not loving. It was a cold, despairing and unhappy place for a boy of six. Not that I was abused or ill fed. To the contrary, my father was relatively well-off financially and had provided an attractive home for Mother and me. Until recently, he had shared it with us.

I hadn't realized we lived in a home devoid of love. For love had fled from my parents' relationship (indeed if it ever existed), to be replaced by hurt and anger. In my mother's case, there was another man, the only male, including myself, that mattered to her, for my birth, as far as she was concerned, had been an error of nature, something to be endured.

My father was a decent man but embittered by events that deprived him of his wife. I believe he unconsciously blamed me. Instead of tightening the bond between them, I had become a source of constant irritation. The shrill arguments and occasional sobs disrupting my sleep were beyond my comprehension. My world was being shattered and thrusting me toward a disaster I could do nothing about. Divorce was agreed upon, with Father transferring his business to a distant city, the house being sold and the problem of my care being settled by the decision to send me to boarding school.

Southside School for Boys was to be my new home. It was a terrifying place, especially for a boy of 6 years who was the youngest boarder. For days Mother assured me that going to Southside was a privilege few other boys enjoyed. I would, she explained, be living with other boys so there would always be playmates. Besides that, Southside would provide me with a fine education few parents could afford. One day I would thank her for the opportunity she'd provided. As the taxi swept up the broad driveway, I caught my first view of the sandstone structure that would be my new home. Windows looking like dead eyes glared out upon deserted playing fields. The only life appeared to be a man mowing with a horse drawn machine. Hating the look of the place, I pulled my suitcase against me for comfort as it contained all my personal possessions. These things would provide some link with my former life that seemed to die with each turn of the taxi's wheels.

Getting out of the taxi, we walked to the foot of a flight of stairs leading to massive wooden doors. The driver carried my heavy suitcase to the landing and rang the doorbell. It opened, revealing a severe-looking woman who announced herself as Mrs. Strongitharm, the matron. "Follow me, please," she ordered curtly. "I'll take you to the Colonel's study."

A great booming voice, responding to her timid knock on the door, bade us enter. A massive man strode forward, informing us in a thunderous voice he was Colonel Allison, headmaster. Expressing delight at seeing my mother again, he thrust a giant hand in my direction, stating he had heard a great deal about me and was sure we would get along splendidly. Intimidated by his size and bluster, I made myself as small as possible behind my mother's back.

"Richard, don't be so silly," she snapped. "This is your headmaster, Colonel Allison. Shake hands like a good boy and make me proud of you. I've told him what a manly, brave boy you are." I didn't feel manly or brave. I felt very small and frightened.

Mother refused the tea offered, explaining she had a taxi waiting. Preparing to leave by the door we'd so recently entered, Mother stopped briefly, gave me a perfunctory kiss, smiled and, urging me to be a good, brave boy, said, "I'll see you during the Christmas holidays," before vanishing into the waiting car.

I cried myself to sleep. The dormitory I occupied had nine other beds but I was the only occupant. My roommates, the matron said, would be arriving tomorrow.

So began years of outright misery relieved only by the sports activities I loved. The routine rarely changed. Roused from bed at six-thirty, allowed half an hour to make beds and have the compulsory cold shower. Breakfast with its porridge, toast and milk. Lessons commencing promptly at eight-thirty with the influx of the day boys, to whom boarders felt superior, but secretly envied. At ten-thirty we broke for sports. Depending upon one's age and the time of year it might be soccer, rugby, hockey, track and field, boxing or cricket.

Lessons resumed promptly at one. All students learned the subjects taught in public schools, plus being exposed to the study of Latin, French and Greek. Strict discipline was enforced by whips called "canes". A caning could be provoked by the slightest misdemeanor: talking in class, eating candy, even a less than satisfactory answer to a question. The unfortunate boy would march to the front of the class, be ordered to touch his toes, and receive shockingly painful swipes across his buttocks. Protesting or crying warranted more brutal punishment.

Severe canings were given for more serious crimes, such as talking in the dormitory after dark. These were excruciatingly painful as they often consisted of "six of the best" across buttocks clad in pajamas. The indignity of the procedure was the expectation of the punisher to be "thanked" for his service. Black and blue welts, days after the event, acted as a mute but graphic reminder of one's sins.

Lessons continued until four in the afternoon when there was a half-hour break before supper, usually a meager meal. Then, we trooped into our classroom for homework. At six years of age I studied for an hour. The older boys could expect to double or triple this period.

The only free time was the hour before bed when the gymnasium was open and the recreational room could be used to listen to the radio or read. It was a Spartan, tough life for all, especially the younger boys like myself.

Although in Canada, Southside was modeled after the English Public School system. Older boys were appointed prefects. When there wasn't a teacher around, they could administer punishments at their discretion.

Bullying was a way of life. Two brothers were the main culprits, making life a living hell for those who resisted their command. One of their favorite pastimes was locking an unfortunate victim under a vaulting horse, then sweeping dust from the dirty floor through the cracks until he choked.

These events couldn't be reported as one would then reap the whirlwind of being branded "a snitch," a title disbarring you from association with other boys. Nor could one complain in a letter home. All letters were monitored by school staff for content and spelling.

I struggled through the fall semester in anticipation of the Christmas holiday. Mrs. Dunne was the only joy in my school life other than the sports. Somehow, word spread in the school that my parents were divorced. I didn't know why, but it created a stigma I couldn't escape. "Your parents are divorced... your parents are divorced", the chant sounded as accusing fingers pointed. I really didn't understand what divorce was but realized it was something to do with my parents no longer living together.

Nothing in my school days upset me as much as this unfathomable hazing. Uncontrollable tears signaled my inner hurt. Mrs. Dunne, obviously aware of my dilemma, pulled me into her classroom after one such incident, closed the door, wiped away my tears, and hugged me tightly. "The boys don't understand what they're saying," she explained. "They're merely parroting the remarks of their cruel and narrow-minded parents." I didn't understand, but realized I had a good friend at Southside.

Only days separated us from the Christmas break. My spirits soared. The cloud of depression, my constant companion for four months, began dissipating. Risking punishment, we talked in excited whispers in the dormitory. Even the masters (the name given all male teachers, except for Colonel Allison, who was called the "Head") seemed to have relaxed their sternness. They also looked forward to the three-week break. I heard Mr. Rice-Jones remark to Mr. Storey, the Latin master, "Just to get away from those little blighters will be holiday enough for me."

We were ordered to have our bags packed by Friday noon as our parents would be picking us up between one and three. We were all dressed in what was called "number one dress": school blazer and tie, gray flannels for those twelve years and over, gray shorts with knee socks, bearing the white and green school colors, for the remainder.

Laughter filled the recreational room and a sense of good fellowship, even from the bullies, permeated the usually somber setting. With soaring hopes I heard the doorbell ring, indicating more parents arriving, followed by disappointment when a name other than mine was called. Eventually there were only three boys left. Then my name was called. Dashing to the front hall, suitcase in hand, filled with bursting anticipation, I was stopped by a grave-looking Colonel Allison. "I'd like to speak to you for a moment in my study, Nelson" he said, not unkindly. Meekly I followed him into his inner sanctum, wondering what could be wrong.

He cleared his throat before speaking. "Sometimes in life, young Nelson, we have to face disappointments. But the person that can rise above his disappointment, like a real man, is the person who will succeed in life. And I think you have the stuff in you to do so."

He paused, pulled a large handkerchief from his pocket, blew his nose lustily, then continued. "I received a phone call from your mother not ten minutes ago and, I'm very sorry to tell you, she will be unable to have you home during the holidays. It seems that things have cropped up making it impossible. She assures me she is very sorry, and will be sending many presents to make you happy...."

The floor seemed to collapse beneath me. I was being whirled around as if in the eye of a cyclone. The room spun crazily with the Colonel and his massive desk seemingly changing places. Tears, hot and stinging, flooded down my cheeks. Wheezing sobs I couldn't control filled the silence of a shattered dream. I was vaguely aware that someone had entered the room to stand beside the Colonel.

The Colonel's voice broke through the misery of rejection that covered me like a sheathing of ice. "I can understand how you feel, Richard," (it was the first time I had ever heard him use my first name) "but we are going to try and make your holidays pleasant. Mrs. Dunne has offered to take you home with her." Only then was I aware it was she who stood beside Colonel Allison, tears in her kindly eyes. "But I don't want to go with Mrs. Dunne!" I screamed. "I want to go to my mother."

Time and gentle persuasion finally brought back some sense of reality, although I felt emotionally withered. Mrs. Dunne held me tightly while wiping away my tears, insisting my mother was probably as upset as I was. She promised I would enjoy myself with her, husband Fred, and their two daughters. My mother or father, she offered, would perhaps do better at the Easter holidays.

Mrs. Dunne was as good as her word. My holidays spent with her family passed in great happiness. Her elder daughter, Marjory, was lovely. Although only eight herself, she treated me as if she were a loving sister. I didn't particularly like either Mrs. Dunne's husband Fred, or Phyllis, who seemed to resent my intrusion into their lives.

I must have been a burden to the family so crowded in a small apartment. Fred, a war veteran, had been gassed and couldn't work. The small salary received by Mrs. Dunne could provide little in the way of luxuries. Nevertheless, that Christmas cemented a bond between Mrs. Dunne and me that I treasured throughout my life.

My youth passed in the seemingly endless days of childhood with only the occasional sunlit peak in valleys of dark despair. The holidays I spent with my mother or father were usually a distorted parody of what I expected. For instance, my mother, now remarried, didn't have time for me. She and her husband, Charles, spent their days entertaining or being entertained. My function seemed to be answering silly questions about Southside, then being totally ignored.

Holidays with Father were equally unsatisfactory. Having found himself a girlfriend, his idea of entertaining me was to have me in his apartment for about a week, then send me to a boys' camp for the remainder of the summer. This was almost like being back at Southside, minus discipline and lessons.

Growing into my teens, the inner humiliation remained disguised by a bluff, exterior bravado. Never would I rely on anybody for love; it only brought sorrow. This determination evaporated immediately when I became infatuated with a girl. Then, puppy-like, I chased her with an unbridled enthusiasm most girls found intimidating. I craved the love I never experienced. I felt guiltily unworthy of affection. I pursued a mirage, a dream, an ideal. My insecurity announced itself like an angry boil in every relationship, making me unpopular. In truth, although I would hotly deny it, I hated myself for being a failure. That my parents had failed, I would never admit. I shouldered the blame and there it remained until finding respite in the wartime Canadian army. I was sixteen.

My trip back in time with Samantha continued. Its realism was complete. I was the young person I'd been. It wasn't merely memory; it was happening.... Now I entered a state of complete comprehension resembling an awakening from a vivid dream. Although still enmeshed in the reality of my unhappy childhood, I was able to view it as an observer, thus allowing another dimension to imprint itself on the periphery of my mind. This was some sort of multi-faceted learning process.

Not only was I feeling all the emotions I had experienced during my young life, but now I am experiencing the emotions of others who interacted with me. Mrs. Dunne, for instance. I can feel her angry sorrow as she invites me to spend Christmas with her family. I can feel her joy when, upon returning to school, I hug her and blurt out my feelings, "I wish my mother were like you."

The school scenes faded. Now I'm preparing to join the army by faking a schoolmate's birth certificate showing me to be eighteen. Then an extraordinary thing....the scene changes... visions of children, boys and girls, who are experiencing the same emotional assassination I'm experiencing, passing before my eyes in painful succession. They are, in one way or another, rejected by one or more of their parents. These are fleeting glimpses, to be sure, but as rapidly as they pass before my eyes, I can feel the torment they produce.

At first I can't see any point in these glimpses of misery. The children seemed to have lived in different ages and cultures without connection. Then comes the realization that there is a common thread. In each case the children's anguish is caused by the lack of love of a parent. My initial puzzlement turns to horror as I realize the connection. I've always been the parent involved.

The scene changes completely. I retrace my last earthly life again. I've joined the army and for the first time feel secure. The army is my home; I belong. It becomes both a mother and father. Its rules are simple and uncompromising. It treats us alike. The army will feed and clothe me, care for me if I become ill, reward me when I work hard. Unlike so many young men who give up lives they love to serve their country, I give up nothing. Only the nightmare that I'm grateful to escape.

CHAPTER 7

Head over Heels

Her uniform didn't disguise her shapely figure as she waited for coffee at the Salvation Army recreational center. I moved beside her. I hadn't seen her face, just her light, brownish hair. She turned as I reached for the container of sugar, sarcasm shading her tone, "I'll pass you the sugar, Corporal. There's no need to stick your arm in my face."

Our eyes met. A feeling like an electric shock coursed through my body. Her eyes belied her belligerence; they were gorgeous, reminding me of a frightened doe. The windows of her soul instinctively signaled a message: "I'm trying to appear worldly.... But I'm really a child, vulnerable, scared of life and looking for protection and love." My instinctive judgement later proved correct.

At the time I didn't analyze my feelings as events unfolded. The advantage of reliving my life was the heightened depth of awareness. In 1943 I'd perceived events through the fresh, adventurous perceptions of youth.

This woman standing beside me with her vulnerable sarcasm, her beauty and aloofness, was a challenge to my ego. I wanted her so much, to have her close, to love her and make her mine.

Sonia also joined the army by lying about her age, as I had. She also joined to escape. In her case, it was from a tyrannical father.

I believed the night I met her to be a disaster. When I suggested walking her back to barracks, she laughed, saying she had many better things to do. Crestfallen, I watched her walk out the door into the sub-zero night. Her physical appearance burned itself into my memory cells. Never had any girl enthralled me as much as she.

I was pulled through the gut to my loins, aflame in a captivating, pulsating, irresistible longing for the sarcastic girl who'd refused me.

I fell in love during that brief encounter. Sonia's being was stamped indelibly on my mind. Those doe-like eyes, mirroring fear and distrust, yet promising unbridled love, seared into my soul. She dominated my being.

That night I couldn't sleep as her image filled my mind. I fantasized wonderful relationships. I recalled her fragrance, or was the fragrance only imagination? Perhaps it was perfume. Maybe it was some primitive signal, yet undiscovered by science, some inner chemistry drawing people together.

Twice the following day I saw her, once with her platoon on morning inspection. Later, I saw her driving a staff car flying a Brigadier's pennant. Each time I became more determined to know her. My opportunity came the following Saturday evening.

Occasionally, the training center held a dance for all ranks in a drill hall. Many troops ignored the army women, preferring instead to date the civilian girls who were always in plentiful supply. Most army girls occupied chairs beside the dance floor, and Sonia was with them.

My dancing ability was like an army truck, rough and ready. Because of this, I'd downed a couple of quick beers to provide the necessary courage to request a dance. With trepidation I approached Sonia, remembering her previous sarcasm. Now, however, there wasn't a trace; only a smile and the assurance she'd love to dance.

We jostled our way about the crowded floor in laughter, for her dancing prowess matched mine. It didn't matter to me, nor did it seem to bother Sonia. All I could think of were those beautiful eyes gazing into mine, and the closeness of her body.

The night flew by on wings of happiness. It was as if nobody else existed. A couple of times others tried to cut in. Sonia used the same excuse: we were going to end this dance together as she had to report to the motor pool immediately for duty.

I walked her through the snow to the barrier leading to the women's quarters. I kissed her goodnight in a lingering closeness of passion, our bodies seeming to merge. I walked back to my hut in a dream as Sonia permeated my being.

Sleep was difficult. Sonia's memory dominated my mind. Every moment we'd been together replayed itself like a film. The distance between us became an ocean, though it was less than a quarter mile. This is stupid, I told myself; I'll see her tomorrow.

Was it love? I'd heard the expression. I didn't know what it meant. But this I realized: never had a woman meant so much. Never had anyone meant as much, including my mother and father. She lingered in my mind as the night lightened into the raucous sound of reveille. But just before the blare of the bugle, I must have slept, for I dreamed.

Sonia was in my dream but no longer in uniform. She was my wife. Her name was Gretchen. We had three children and lived in a small town in Bavaria. I was still a soldier, but a German soldier, on leave due to wounds received at Ypres. My pass from my regiment was dated January 8, 1917.

Most dreams fade like wispy clouds in a gale force wind. Not this one. Even in the rush of the morning's duties, the dream persisted in brilliant reality.

Sonia and I planned to meet that night at the Salvation Army hut, the army's wonderful oasis of cheap coffee, doughnuts and free movies. Waiting anxiously until she entered, I saw her pause to scan the crowded room. My wave produced a smile and signal of acknowledgment. Admiringly, I watched her flowing grace as she approached the table. She is, I thought, the most gorgeous girl I've known.

We drank coffee until show time. The picture was awful. Cowboys with continuously loaded revolvers shooting treacherous Indians in a grainy twilight of thundering hooves. We held hands and whispered until a rough voice asked us to shut up. Excusing ourselves, we tripped our way over a dozen sets of legs to find the canteen practically deserted. We talked.

I was just about to tell Sonia about my dream, as it still floated around the periphery of my memory. She beat me to the punch. It also concerned a dream she'd had last night. "It's completely crazy," she'd said. "You were a German soldier, a corporal as you are now, and you'd been badly wounded in an attack by Canadian soldiers at a place you called Ypres. Your name was Gerhard and I was your wife."

I almost spilled my coffee as I leaned toward her. "And," I asked, "do you know what your name was in your dream?" "Oh, sure. My name was Gretchen," she laughed. And blushing slightly, she continued, "We had three kids."

CHAPTER 8

Shadow of Death

Sonia and I both realized our time together was short. Soon I'd be fighting, as twice I'd requested an overseas posting. Now my request had been granted. I would leave with the next draft, as soon as enough troops completed their training.

We sometimes discussed what we'd do when the war ended. There wasn't the slightest doubt in either of our minds that we'd be on the winning side. I suspected that one day I'd become a writer or maybe attend university. Possibly I'd make the regular army my career. Sonia liked the former choices much better. She didn't much relish the discipline the Women's Army Corps imposed on her lifestyle.

We talked of marriage after the war. Whether this would have succeeded is open to conjecture, for we were both young, inexperienced and idealistic.

Life seemed to stretch into infinity, a never-ending adventure. Even the prospect of battle didn't raise the thought of my life being terminated. This was strange, as all my training was directed toward killing. It wasn't until I took part in battle that the possibility of my death became real. Training continued as we waited to go overseas. Our company marched 25 miles to bivouac and receive live ammunition training. This meant we would cross ground while machine gun fire was directed overhead. It provided a taste of the battles we would face.

Being an instructor, I'd experienced this many times. I suspected that, as usual, at least one soldier would panic. Once, the man ahead of me was shot through the buttocks. Another time it was more serious. Crawling along the shallow ditch with lead screaming overhead, a man jumped to his feet just as an explosive charge was detonated to simulate artillery or mortar fire. He was killed instantly.

Near the bivouac area was a community hall built of logs. In peacetime this forested area was a popular camping and picnic ground. It nestled into its stream-side setting of pines with a backdrop of soaring mountain peaks.

Our commandant arranged a dance Saturday night. Transport was provided for volunteers from the Women's Army Corps. I knew Sonia would be among them if she wasn't on duty.

With a sinking feeling I watched as more than twenty girls jumped from the back of the truck. I asked one if she knew where Sonia was. To my relief, she replied she was on the second truck, due to arrive in about ten minutes.

That night was memorable to me, cloudless and relatively warm, the air filled with the scent of pine trees and burning wood fires. Groups gathering together to talk or sing. From the community hall came the sound of music, "I'll Be Seeing You," "Elmer's Tune," "Deep in The Heart of Texas,"....

Overhead a star canopy of brilliance twinkled through the tree branches. During lulls in conversation or music, the quiet murmuring of the stream could be heard, softly grumbling its way to the ocean.

It was a night for young love, a magical time searing itself into my subconscious memories, always summoned back to consciousness by a hint of its ingredients: a starry night, the smell of pine, one of the melodies.

Return Passage

Holding Sonia in my arms, I was oblivious to time or space; she was both... my universe, my destiny. Neither of us had any way of knowing how fragile our universe was.

Just after midnight, the two-truck convoy of girls departed. A brilliant moon enabled us to see as if it were daylight. Sonia pushed her way to a tailgate position, her cap pushed back, her eyes sparkling with animation and love. In the hubbub of noise, I really couldn't hear what she was saying as the trucks moved away, but I could read her lips. She said, "I love you, Darling."

Then she was gone. I watched until the single red taillight faded into the distance. A hush fell over the forest of pine as a hundred and twenty soldiers headed for their blankets and sleep.

Sunday routine was practically the same as any other day with one exception: we had to attend church. The Canadian Army only recognized three religions: Roman Catholic, Anglican or Jewish.

The church service in the bivouac area was mercifully short because our company commander ordered, "Make it brief, Padre; we've got to get these god damned exercises over before tomorrow night."

Word spread through the ranks, although I was almost the last to hear. The women returning to camp had had trouble. The second truck ran off the gravel road into a ditch. Some girls were injured, one seriously.

I was worried although there was no great apprehension, no sudden illumination of fact, just a dull worry that Sonia may have been hurt. Sunday and Monday passed quickly and, as there was no further word about the accident, my worries began to fade.

We marched and doubled the 25 miles back to camp in 90 degree temperature. I showered, put on a clean uniform and headed for the Women's Army Corps barrier. I requested the picket to summon Sonia. As I waited, I realized, once again, how much Sonia meant to me. I loved her more than anything else in this world.

The routine at the barrier was simple. The picket took the name of the girl wanted, entered the small sentry box to telephone on the direct line to the women's orderly room. The duty NCO dispatched a runner to the women's quarters. I thought the picket gave me a strange look when I mentioned Sonia. I waited about five minutes, not unusual due to the lack of a paging system. Instead of Sonia, two other women approached the barrier: a lieutenant, wearing the Orderly Officer arm band, accompanied by the Women's Army Corps company commander, Major Greer.

I saluted, expecting them to pass by. Instead, Major Greer addressed me. "You are Corporal Nelson, I presume?" I assured her I was. "Will you come with us, please, Corporal." It was a command as she was a major and I a corporal.

Mystified, I accompanied them to their administration building. Major Greer sat at her desk and waved me to a chair opposite her. My brain raced to find some logical explanation of this strange procedure. Was Sonia pregnant?

"Your first name is Richard, isn't it?" I nodded. "I'm afraid I have some very sad news, Richard." The use of my first name set alarm bells ringing. "I believe that you and Lance Corporal Sommers were very close." I nodded again, my throat tightening, and my mouth becoming dry. "She was a fine young woman and a very good soldier...." Numbness swept through my brain, the room turned like a giant Wurlitzer, sweat coursed down my body. Was. . . was. . . a fine soldier. What was Major Greer talking about?

"Where is Sonia?" I demanded. An infuriating silence lingered in the still office. "Where is she, please, Ma'am?" I repeated, jumping to my feet and leaning across the desk.

Major Greer rose, came around the desk and placing both hands on my shoulders, said, "I'm so very sorry to have to tell you, Richard, that Corporal Sommers died in military hospital this afternoon." Black misery sucked me downward into a world of disbelief and denial. Anger flared, engulfing me in a shrieking damnation of anything worthwhile or good. Sonia filled every memory cell; intense feelings, a thousand pictures, a welling tenderness... torn asunder, gone forever.

Hatred burned like ignited gas, a killing, murdering anger, unbridled rage directed at whoever was responsible: people, things or the God who permitted such a happening..... Yes, especially God. That unknown monster who would permit such a desecration of sweetness, goodness and beauty.

I can scarcely remember the remainder of that evening. I had been raised in an era that taught men shouldn't cry. I did. The tears crested like a waterfall to be followed by dry, racking sobs.

Vaguely I recall Major Greer sympathetically placing her arms around me. The Orderly Officer made a phone call; my company commander and the Protestant Padre appeared.

The Padre spoke about everlasting life and God caring about each of His creations. My Major talked about life and death, emphasizing — if my recollection is correct — the role of the soldier and the greater suffering I would encounter overseas. He used flattery, saying I was a soldier he felt would be a credit to him and his Company.

The days that followed were the worst I'd ever experienced. Every thought was with Sonia. I scarcely slept. I went through my duties in a fog of misery. Capping everything else was Sonia's military funeral.

The finality of the volley of rifle fire over her grave. The mournful bugle notes sounding Retreat and Reveille. The Padre intoning solemnly about a valley of death that Sonia would walk to reach eternal life.

I stood alone at the freshly covered grave as the funeral party departed. My darling, her neck broken because some driver had been careless and run the wheels off the side of the road.

A kid of seventeen whose life had been misery. Her father stupid, uncaring and brutal. Her mother, once pretty, brought to a foreign country, unable to communicate in English, totally dependent upon her gross, tyrannical husband. The only outlet for his frustrations and failures was the subjection of the two people closest to him. One of whom was Sonia.

Return Passage

I walked away past the rows of headstones. Those buried there, I thought, had loved, had been loved and by their departure from this life had given birth to the emotions of despair now engulfing me. Was there really, as the Padre had said, another life in a place called Heaven? Was Sonia on a journey to a better existence? Or, was it more realistic to think that this promise was just a way of making people feel better?

Into my shroud of black despair, occasionally, would flash a mystical thought that perhaps those who talked of a life hereafter were correct. But these thoughts were rare and short-lived.

CHAPTER 9

Ghosts and God

I relived my life in a clarity of understanding impossible in the earth state. With equal poignancy, I experienced my emotions and the effect my actions had upon others. I felt their emotional response as keenly as I felt my own.

I relived the moment of my death that now seemed like a familiar departure gate for a more interesting future. From the fury and fear of battle, the cold and icy mud of the Schelde, I opened my eyes to the lovely gaze of Samantha.

"Welcome home, Richard," she smiled. I returned to the present in the way station with a far greater understanding of how my actions had affected others as we intermingled in life.

I told her that although I had no doubt increased my knowledge, the reliving of my last life gave me the feeling of barely scratching the whole truth, of knowing so little. Samantha listened carefully as I tried to convey my feelings.

"This understanding of yours, Richard — the fact that you now are aware how ignorant we are of the universal plan — is the beginning of knowledge. We will never have complete knowledge, either. We are capable of knowing only so much, at any one time. However," she laughed, "it really doesn't matter. As long as we know that all of us are a part of creation and, therefore, a part of the Creator, we will be infinitely wiser."

I asked Samantha if death were an illusion. She assured me that this was correct. "There are souls, however," she said, "that even in their higher dimension choose not to seek the light of truth. In other words, they are souls who turn their backs on the Creator to pursue paths of their own choosing."

"Some of these beings," Samantha explained, "are so tied to the earth vibration that they try to remain perpetually in its sphere. These unfortunates run the gamut from being harmless earthbound spirits who refuse to move into a higher plane," she said sorrowfully, "to others under the influence of evil creatures of higher stature."

"Can both the harmless and evil earthbound spirits materialize as the so-called ghosts and apparitions we spoke of on earth?" I asked. She gave an affirmative answer. "Isn't it strange," she continued, "how so many of us have doubts about an afterlife while in bodily form?" I agreed, thinking of how I felt losing Sonia. "Yet the evidence that physical death isn't the end is all around us. Thousands of reliable, sober and trustworthy people in every generation give testimony to having some experience with spirit forms."

I hadn't thought about the things she was saying. But she was correct. There were many stories I had heard from absolutely reliable people, such as the family I'd met while training in England.

During the Battle of Britain a German bomber had been shot down and crashed in a wood not far from their house. The entire crew died and their bodies had been interred in the local cemetery.

Eric, recently discharged from the British Army because of severe wounds received in North Africa, took pleasure in walking his yellow Labrador retriever through the numerous pathways weaving their way through the trees.

The dog, true to breed, was a playful, gentle animal, well trained and obedient to command. There was one thing she utterly refused to do. She wouldn't walk through a particular glade in the forest. This annoyed Eric, who forcefully attempted to drag the dog by her collar.

"The dog absolutely refused to go through the glade," explained Eric. "I dragged her until she began to choke. Whenever we reached this particular location, the fur on her back rose, her tail would go between her legs, she'd whimper and try desperately to run in the opposite direction." If not leashed, she would turn tail, oblivious to Eric's shouts, and run home. Eric was bewildered by the dog's behavior.

Eric and his wife, Pat, were new to the Petworth area. Their London home had been bombed during the blitz. When an opportunity to buy the attractive old cottage had presented itself, they jumped at the opportunity. Eric knew nothing about the crash of a German bomber that occurred three years before. It wasn't until he visited the local pub and mentioned the strange behavior of his dog that the crash of the German bomber and death of its crew was mentioned. The pub owner asked the precise location. Eric drew a rough map with pencil and paper. "That be the spot that German bomber came down," the publican said.

Briefly I told Samantha of this strange event. She nodded. "You know, Richard, how difficult it is to accept the fact of physical death. Fortunately, you had an open mind. Some individuals are not so fortunate. The crew of that bomber, for instance.

"They were probably relatively young, as you yourself were. They most likely had a markedly different upbringing, Hitler youth, perhaps. Probably indoctrinated to believe they were superior men, engaged in a holy war for the Fatherland, immune to death. Probably one or more refused to accept the fact of their death. Bewildered, they hang around the crash site long after their bodies and the wreckage have been removed. What you don't understand is this. In spirit form there is no such thing as time as we know it in physical life. Days, months, years, even centuries, mean nothing." I would question her on this astounding idea later.

"But what about the dog?" I wanted to know. "Animals have the ability to sense what most humans can't," she explained. "The dog could feel the energy field of those spirit beings, particularly if they were highly agitated. If they had been at peace, the dog may not have reacted. Naturally, some humans also have the ability to sense spirit forms. These are the mediums, psychics or sensitives." She laughed, "They go by many names."

This story brought back another I knew to be authentic. It was told me by a man who claimed to be an atheist. He was my father.

During World War One, my dad, then a captain, had been badly wounded. He was recuperating in a stately country home in England that had been volunteered for this service.

One afternoon he sat in the garden with the aristocratic owner, a lady whose husband was an officer serving in France. The woman's large dog lay napping at her feet. Suddenly, the dog looked up, jumped to his feet and, barking joyfully, ran to the iron gate.

He leapt into the air repeatedly, as if trying to place his paws on somebody's shoulders.

The lady remarked how strange her dog's actions were. He always did this, she said, when her husband returned home. It was a routine repeated every day prior to hostilities.

The dog's joy was evident. He bounded along toward the woman and my father, giving small yelps of obvious pleasure and then sat staring at an empty chair beside the table. Occasionally he raised his paw as if expecting it to be shaken. The woman remarked how strangely her dog was acting. "It is exactly how he used to act when George arrived."

The following day a telegram arrived from the War Office regretfully informing her that her husband had been killed in action. Had the dead officer come home? Had he been sitting in the chair?

"There's really no way of telling now," Samantha said, "but it's very likely. Spirits often return to the ones they love after death. However, they find they can't communicate." "Is it true, Samantha, that all dogs possess a faculty we humans no longer have?"

She nodded. "Is it because a dog that is loved worships its master?" I asked.

"I suppose you could say so," Samantha answered thoughtfully. "Great love is a form of worship, isn't it?"

The word "worship" was one I rarely used. In a way, I guess, I worshiped Sonia. No, that was wrong. I loved her greatly. "Worship" was a word reserved for God.

Worship was something we did in church. We worshiped God. Worship was a concept I'd always found difficult. What did we worship? I couldn't visualize God or Jesus Christ, who, believers say, was God in the flesh.

He was the Creator incarnate, whose suffering, torment and rejection would clear the way for mankind's salvation, if they believed in Him. I tried very hard to understand and worship. It didn't work. I mentioned my feelings to Samantha with trepidation. I don't know what I feared, but I was fearful of my lack of understanding, my doubts. The jaws of hell emerged from somewhere in my imagination. A burning fury of lost souls, relegated forever to an existence of suffering and torment. You must... worship no other God. The first Commandment.

The softest hands took mine in their gentle grip. Samantha's glorious eyes looked deep into my own. They radiated truth, understanding love, and an appreciation of my inner turmoil, my deep-rooted fears.

She spoke softly. "Dear Richard. What sort of Creator do you think we have? How can we possibly worship something we can't comprehend? The Creator is not some monster who expects absolute obedience from the unknowing. The Creator is not a power that demands blind worship. The Creator loves His creations. God knows our lack of perception and knowledge. Our Creator realizes we will do things foolish and harmful. That is why He allows us to learn by giving us eternal life and many opportunities for spiritual growth.

"God," she continued in her melodious voice, "is many things. Do you think that those people early in our development who worshiped the sun, star formations or nature itself, were wrong? No," she answered herself. "They were worshiping God in a way they could comprehend.

"There are always those amongst us who will rise to prominence. They become our politicians, military leaders, philosophers, scientists and priests. Those in charge will produce dogma, often for preservation of their own power.

"This dogma is often stupid, but very difficult to ignore. Gods have been numerous and varied. Some have been in or out of favor, based on the preferences of those in authority.

"No," she concluded, "God is not the sometimes-selfish deity that is often portrayed. All He demands is that we love what has been created. Love our fellow human beings. And, Richard, that isn't easy, as we all know." Samantha's simplicity was astounding and it made sense.

As a child in Sunday school, I had found the explanations regarding judgment hard to swallow. If you didn't worship God in the correct way, damnation and eternal fire would be your fate. But as I grew older, many concepts bothered me. I'd think of a child brought up wretchedly poor. This child sometimes was abused. He or she could have a brutal, drunken father and a mother who sold her body for drugs.

The grown child might turn to a life of crime, become a drug addict, alcoholic or murderer. This individual didn't have a fair chance. "Would his environment and his lack of proper guidance be taken into account?" I asked.

Samantha assured me that the complete circumstances would be considered as God was completely fair and understanding. "But," she retorted, "have you asked yourself why people are born into circumstances like that?" I had always believed it to be fate. I felt, however, another explanation would be given me later.

I posed another situation. A child is born into a home of wealth and affluence. His parents are devout Christians. Not only is this child privileged, but highly intelligent and knowledgeable. He doesn't need crime to prosper. Due to his fortunate circumstances, he has every opportunity to be generous, kind and good. Is this individual judged by the same criteria as his less fortunate brother or sister? The answer I'd been given to this question was always the same: "God knows."

Even as a child this answer hadn't satisfied me. Nor did the fact that most of the world had never come into contact with the road to salvation, Jesus Christ. Again the same answer was proffered by those who thought they knew. "God is fair; God knows and understands and will make allowances for the fact of their ignorance of the truth."

Sometimes, doubting the religious truths in which I was indoctrinated, I thought it more beneficial if I'd been born in the far reaches of Nepal. By so doing, I would have had a better chance of reaching Heaven and eternal life because of my ignorance of Christian truth.

My thoughts and memories were received by Samantha without need of verbal communication. We were joined by a radiant link of understanding. Was this telepathic communication a natural occurrence in the spiritual realm?

My shallow intellect began to reel. I was totally ignorant of any real knowledge or understanding. Here I was, supposedly dead and in spirit form, talking to a spirit being regarding every fear, thought, memory, feeling and skepticism I've ever encountered. It seemed crazy.

Samantha once again came into focus. Her eyes mirrored love and caring. The logical simplicity of her explanations of the most complex matter were a revelation. The quest for more knowledge burst like a geyser from within. A thousand questions rushed into my mind.

Samantha smiled. "All in good time, Richard. We really do have an eternity to learn things. I believe it's time for Sonia and John to be finished. You and she will have much to discuss."

Samantha was correct; for as soon as she'd finished speaking, I heard Sonia's voice and saw that she still sat facing John. I had been completely oblivious of them. John and Samantha rose to leave. Sonia and I were left alone.

I blurted out the incredible experiences I'd experienced. "I know exactly what you mean," Sonia answered. "I'm experiencing the same thing. And each session sheds more light on the purpose of our creation." She became serious. "Some parts are pretty grim while others are wonderful. It makes us realize how stupid we are. How our purpose in life becomes diffused by our ego and pride in the fleeting world of the flesh."

Sonia told me of the experiences I would have if my education were to follow her format. There would be many lives to relive. There would be group study, just like being back in school, where question and answers are encouraged.

"The guides, although authorities, are certainly not authoritarian. There is no self-righteousness here, like that found in many of the earthly clergy. The teachers here realize, with compassion, the difficulties of bodily life. They've all suffered through it themselves. And many will re-enter the physical plane again to increase their spirituality."

This fascinated me. "I really can't imagine Samantha being human, nor John for that matter," I exclaimed. "Can you?" Sonia tipped her face slightly to one side, and smilingly suggested that I should ask Samantha about it. I promised to do so.

At our next session, with some trepidation, I asked Samantha if she would tell me a little of her past. I didn't know what her response would be. The last thing I wanted was to lessen the rapport I enjoyed with this beautiful Being.

I needn't have worried, for with a radiant smile, she nodded her head. "Of course, Richard. In bodily form we don't go to a medical doctor unless he is qualified, do we? You want my credentials."

CHAPTER 10

The Substance of Samantha

Samantha again asked me to relax as her enchanting tones lulled me into another dimension. This time things were different. Instead of experiencing the pain and trauma of events in my own life, I watched in fascination as another soul's journey was unfolded before my eyes. The events unfolded quickly like a fantastic three-dimensional movie. The soul, I realized, was Samantha.

A poor farmer with many children labored under a hot sun. His dwelling was a crude hut made of baked mud and straw. The family eked out a fragile living, barely having enough food to sustain themselves. Half of everything they grew was commandeered by their ruler, who lived in lavish opulence. The farmer, a kindly man, lived to be forty-two, and died believing that his god Osiris would enable him to enter the realm of Amenti.

Then, the soul that developed into Samantha became a woman. There was no beauty about her for she was poor and disfigured. Her life was one of starvation, cold and squalor. The few scraps of food that sustained her were sometimes shared with a blind mongrel dog. Almost mercifully, she died in agony, alone and uncared for. The only thing that noted her passing was the loneliness of the little dog.

Again, Samantha was a woman but this time she possessed much of the beauty she now possessed. Life was good for she'd been born into a wealthy family of power. She was one of three sisters, the youngest, and was her father's favorite. She married an eligible bachelor also from a wealthy, influential family. Soon, she became mother of twin girls and a boy.

Life seemed ideal. They possessed all luxuries. The husband was kind and considerate and the young wife enjoyed the prestige of her position. But then something went horribly wrong. The woman's character changed.

She became suspicious of her husband's loyalty, without cause. Personal servants, with whom she had previously shared a pleasant relationship, were now accused of spying and summarily dismissed from service.

She withdrew further into a world of fear and self-pity, finding fault with all those who loved her. No longer did she care about herself, becoming disheveled and dirty. The best doctors were summoned, but their treatments only exacerbated the problem.

Priests were called for exorcism, as it was now thought she was possessed of evil spirits. But this only made matters worse. Convinced that his once beautiful wife was beyond help, the resigned young husband heeded the advice he was now given. He had her confined to a locked room in a distant wing of their mansion. At first she screamed incessantly. Then, refusing all food, she became gaunt and skeletal. Gradually she fell into a deep coma. Soon she was dead.

The next body Samantha entered was that of a child, a handsome little boy. Life at first was joyful as he was loved and pampered by adoring parents. This ideal situation came to an abrupt end when both parents were killed in a fire.

The boy was then sheltered by an aunt and uncle who felt that fate had dealt them a blow by adding additional responsibility upon their shoulders. Brought up within the family without being part of it, he found himself being singled out for all the unpleasant duties. His obvious superiority in both physical appearance and mental ability infuriated his cousins, who joined their parents in their growing disenchantment with him.

The boy, however, seemed to shrug off his unpleasant situation and returned kindness for abuse. His intellect was appreciated by those he came in contact with outside his immediate family. As he approached manhood he was selected for higher education, preparing him for positions of responsibility in government.

He soon became a leading figure in the Spanish establishment, far surpassing the stature of his uncle and his cousins. Because of his success, his adoptive family feigned friendship. Inwardly, their envy of him turned to hatred. Hard times befell his relatives. He immediately provided the money and influence to re-establish their shattered fortune. Outwardly their gratitude was boundless. Inwardly, their hatred of him increased.

The Inquisition was at its peak. The soul who became Samantha was not a deeply religious man, although a loyal Roman Catholic. Among friends he expressed his disgust with the actions of the Inquisitors, calling them repressive and cruel. His uncle and cousins seized upon this as a method of revenge.

So it was that at the zenith of his success, he was arrested and charged with heresy. This accusation was without foundation, other than his criticism of the Inquisition itself.

To his dismay he discovered the main witnesses for the prosecution were his uncle, aunt and cousins, who, in brutal testimony, accused him of the most heinous crimes against the mother church. He was tortured, convicted and executed.

Samantha lived many more lives, some successful and happy, many wretched. In some, the body her soul inhabited was healthy and handsome. In others she was ugly and sickly. Sometimes she lived a full life. At other times her life was terminated by accident or illness. Sometimes she was intelligent, in other lives she appeared dull and stupid. The episodes of her many incarnations flowed by with only one discernible theme: each existence, in some way, seemed to enable Samantha's soul to have an experience that would be of benefit. If, in one life she was haughty and proud, inevitably in the lifetime following she would be humbled.

Samantha had experienced almost every conceivable situation, from being a lowly prostitute to a high ranking cleric. Strangely enough, she had become a prostitute in the life following her successful career in the church. She chose this life because, as she had acknowledged, she had lacked understanding and pity.

I was given the privilege of seeing how Samantha chose which earthly existence would be of most benefit. A council of highly evolved souls discussed the progress, or lack of it, her last life had produced. Then, with infinite wisdom and loving kindness, they made the recommendations for another earth life which would probably be of most benefit in the development of Samantha's soul.

The final choice of whether or not to follow the set of circumstances that would probably result in a particular lifetime was left to Samantha to decide. Her guides would only suggest she follow a route they considered advantageous. Usually, their suggestions proved to be the correct course to follow, but not always. Free will was always in evidence, permitting Samantha to journey from the path she wished to. Sometimes this was beneficial; often it was not.

Being allowed to see Samantha's journey through many lifetimes taught me the meaning of infinity. This gave me a joyful new perspective, shattering the illusions of a one lifetime, make-it-or-break-it proposition as espoused by some of the great earthly religions.

In the final, quick phases of Samantha's journey as a human entity, I noted the great progress she had made in her spiritual development. There had been episodes of her earthbound journey when she had faltered. Always, however, the opportunity had been given her to learn from her mistakes.

Some lessons, in human time, were long and difficult. In infinity, I realized, their duration could be compared to a flash of lightning. A series of lifetimes, in fact, lasted no longer than the dying echo of thunder. As Samantha progressed, I saw great change. Love and caring for others became her obsession. This was not relegated to her fellow human beings exclusively, for she loved the earth and all its creatures. She learned that everything created was joined by a common bond, the bond of the Creator's love.

CHAPTER 11

Reaping What's Sown

"Are you ready to experience another existence?" Samantha asked. "The rerun of your most recent life was to enhance your memory. Soon we'll be exploring your other past lives to judge how much progress you've made in becoming one with our Creator. The Creator doesn't predestine events. He allows us to follow the path of our own choosing in making the correct decisions for spiritual advancement. The possibilities of success are always present, although often we fail to take advantage of them due to our worldly perspective."

Something clicked in my mind, the East Indian belief in reincarnation. I recalled many world religions believed mankinds' struggles were based on the theory of rebirth. I searched my memory for the word associated with reincarnation.

Karma, that was the word. I asked Samantha if this had a bearing on what I would be experiencing. Her perfection of a smile radiated its warmth, "Oh yes, Richard, karma is the reason we all must experience the things we do over many lifetimes.

"Being raised a Christian, you'll remember hearing, 'As you sow, so shall you reap.' That is the explanation of karma. There is nothing more to say." My puzzlement relit the radiance of her smile. "You saw how my lives intertwined with the lives of others.

Sometimes I had to pay debts or learn hard lessons. You remember I became a prostitute after my lifetime as a high-ranking cleric?

"Unfortunately, in Christianity karma is misunderstood. Christians are taught that reaping consequences applies to a nebulous hereafter after death. Those who place their faith in Jesus Christ will have everlasting life. Those who don't will suffer an eternity of suffering."

I understood her for I'd occasionally heard a Reverend Abraham on radio. His sermons inevitably focused on the fire, brimstone and suffering of hell. He frequently implied that a donation mailed to him would be of great help in escaping this fate.

"This place, this halfway house, isn't exclusively for Christians, or is it, Samantha?" I asked, immediately feeling foolish. Major MacDougal, I knew, was a confessed atheist while I'd stayed as far away from church as possible.

"Heavens, no." The sunrise of a smile revealed her perfect teeth. "Christians are a distinct minority here. But let me qualify that statement by saying true Christians who adhere to Christ's teaching, true Buddhists, Hindus or Muslims who followed the teaching of their Masters, have progressed far more than others.

"Each doctrine is the plan for spiritual development and the Masters have shown the most direct road to the Creator."

I again interrupted, "But can all Masters be correct? Didn't they teach different things? I was taught that the non-Christian religions were created by false prophets or even Satan himself."

"All Masters, Richard, speak the words of the Creator. They say the same thing in the context of their genius and time on earth. All were inspired with the spirit of God...."

My early indoctrination into Christian doctrine rebelled. Samantha was saying things that, I knew, would be labeled as blasphemy. "Jesus is the Light and the Way," the only way, I remembered.

Could she give me a few examples that demonstrated a unity of teaching? Samantha said she could and would. "Do you remember your Bible?" she asked. "Not too well," I admitted. "Never mind. I'm sure this will ring a bell. It is from the first verse of John.

"'In the beginning was the Word, and the Word was with God, and the Word was God; the same was in the beginning with God.'" I acknowledged this was familiar and Samantha continued. "Here is practically the same thing. 'In the beginning the Lord of the Universe alone existed. With him the word was second, and (the) word is verily the Supreme Brahman.' Brahman is God in their parlance," she explained. "These words are from the Indian Vedas, older than the Bible.

"We spoke earlier of the most important rule Christ gave us: 'Do unto others as you would have others do unto you.' Other religions say the same thing. The Mahabharata said, 'Do not to others what ye do not wish done to yourself; and wish for others to what ye desire and long for, for yourself. This is the whole of righteousness, heed it well.' Another way of putting the same directive is from Zoroaster, who states, 'That which is good for all and anyone, For whomsoever - that is good for me... What I hold good for self, I should for all. Only Law Universal is true law.'"

Samantha paused. "There are many more examples of the duality of religious truths. Many things Jesus said are similar to what other enlightened Masters stated in an earlier age. Some believe Jesus came to earth often. Many early Christians believed he lived as Adam and Elias.

"So you won't get swamped with theories," she laughed, " I'm going to quote what the Upanishads, holy book of the Hindus, has to say. I think you'll agree it makes sense.

"'Cows are of many colors, but milk is of one color, white; So the proclaimers who proclaim the Truth use many varying forms to express it, But yet the Truth enclosed in all is One.'"

She looked into my eyes. "There is really so much to learn, Richard. During each visit here we have to establish the understanding of our journey and hope that some knowledge will carry over in the next incarnation."

Again, the ability to read my mind was evident. Just as I was going to ask why we couldn't retain all knowledge during earth life, she answered, "We don't remember everything in the denser vibration of bodily form because it would inhibit learning.

"In school you're not given a copy of the test or examination you'll be taking. Nor are you allowed to have an expert coaching you from the sidelines. So it is with our earthly journeys; we must work to learn the truth. We must feel the pain, the sorrow, the joy and happiness to remember the lessons.

"You can tell a young child a hot stove will burn him, but until he experiences the actual pain, it doesn't register. That's why we are encouraged to choose a life beneficial in obtaining the lessons we require. You'll remember I chose a lifetime that led me to prostitution. I needed the lesson because in my previous life in the church, I lacked understanding and pity for others.

"Enough for now," she laughed. "We must proceed with the job of experiencing your past lives." Samantha bade me relax as her melodious voice lulled me into another dimension.

CHAPTER 12

Atlantis

Entering the monitor, I strapped on sensors to monitor all bodily functions as the chair adjusted to my physical contours. Soft music filled the cubicle as the subliminal soundtrack, designed to erase all tensions and stresses, entered my subconscious. This weekly routine was mandatory for civil servants. The elite of the populace had to do it less often, once a month was sufficient. The drones were monitored only when they showed signs of malfunctioning.

My mind refused to be calmed. The printed record being received in the Ministry of Health would certainly detect some stress due to elevated blood pressure. My explanation of crisis in my department might suffice. I realized the bureaucrats in the Ministry of Health were hard to convince; a tense employee was a threat to sound, logical, deductive thought.

My mind was on Antuk, the most southerly part of our vast empire. As Deputy Minister of Labor, I was directly responsible for supplying drones to fill the quota necessary for an efficient operation. Somehow, our genetic engineering was failing. Recently we'd received drones of insufficient mental capacity to carry out simple tasks. More alarming, there were other drones with above average intelligence who'd started agitating for political rights.

I wrestled with the problem although I was not responsible. But facts could be twisted, and I realized if any blame was directed at me, it could be wreck my career.

The Ministry demanded perfection. It had taken me nearly five hundred years of hard, devoted work to reach my present level. To protect myself, I initiated steps to ensure the incompetents responsible for genetic failure would pay for their failure. I recorded a message to the Ministry of Science with a duplicate copy for my superiors. I didn't mince words, placing blame on those liable: the Director of Genetic Engineering and his staff.

On my trip home on the Anti-Gravity Transporter my mind was still focused on my actions. This was the first serious glitch in our scientific progress and our success as a nation had been built by scientific achievement. So had Mu's. The two nation-continents, Atlantis and Mu, now coexisted in peace. Brutal warfare and the archaic power struggles, once prevalent, were relegated to the historical videos of 700 years ago.

Science had all but eliminated death, other than by accident. Genetically engineered sub-drones, with only sufficient brain function to keep their organs healthful, were in such plentiful supply that organ transplants were being performed, not only on ourselves, but upon drones.

My home was located in the cool hills of the eastern coast approximately 1000 miles from the capital, an hour's trip by Anti-Gravitator Transporter. I preferred this method of travel as I could view the landscape and relax, an impossibility in the ten minute sub-orbital flight. An attractive female drone met me at the terminus to fly me the final few kilometers. "You're Sinta, aren't you?" I inquired. Sinta, who'd acknowledged her name, was a creation of the BWTBE series of drones. The initials abbreviated their genetic encoding: blond, white, tall, and blue eyed.

I had five days of leisure until the next two-day work period. I had nothing planned but suspected my family would offer some suggestions. I vaguely remembered promising my son to accompany him on his next spaceflight. He spent much of his time in space, having recently joined a club devoted to that pastime. Space within our own solar system now bored me; I'd seen it often. My daughter would spend all her time with her scientist boyfriend, while my wife socialized. If she wasn't surrounded by a group of people, she became introverted and unhappy.

This evening was Terminations Night at the arena, an event, subsidized and encouraged by the government, that we enjoyed. The government's interest was understandable. With physical death a rarity, and war an anachronism of a bygone age, the populace could vent any violent emotions in a humanely controlled environment.

The Terminations provided this outlet. Special drones were bred as gladiators: huge, muscular male giants and beautiful looking females.

The team battles are breathtaking. Each team, garbed in distinctive uniform and armed with the most primitive weapons, is introduced to the roaring approval of their supporters. With flailing arms, like conquering heroes they acknowledge their acclaim.

Facing annihilation, as most do, it is difficult to know their emotions. Their lust for blood is bred over many generations, the product of the earliest genetically engineered drones, those bred to fight in the lower echelons of the armed forces in the days of warfare.

The National Anthem over, the two teams commence battle by advancing in extended lines toward the center of the arena. There, individually, they face their designated adversary in a battle to the death. The game is simple: the winning team will have most survivors.

There are some who decry this form of entertainment, describing it as debased, cruel or barbaric. I disagree; in my knowledge selective breeding has made ritual warfare the vocation they enjoy.

In the days of random birth, cruel, unfeeling and loathsome individuals made murder, robbery and violence their trademark. Successive governments provided penal institutions as a solution that combined all the expertise psychiatry and criminology could provide.

For most criminals it failed. Incarceration seemed only to exacerbate the criminal violence as those so inclined learned from association with others.

Those with sound scientific reasoning stepped forward. With genetic engineering, they argued, it was possible to turn these genes of violence into a national asset. The genes of the brave could be spliced with those of the violent, producing soldiers for the armed forces.

There was great opposition. Old religious beliefs still swayed the superstitious. This procedure would be entering a field reserved for God. This could lead to a super-race mentality. A dictatorial government, they speculated, could use genetic engineering to elevate a highly intelligent ruling class. These prophets of doom were wrong. Women provided the leadership in demanding genetic engineering. As parents, they demanded their offspring to be intelligent, attractive and superior. Sperm banks became commonplace where one could order the size, coloring, characteristics and intelligence of the child.

The child could have all the characteristics wanted, and retain some parental attributes, if desired. It was a matter of splicing in the desirable features of the parents' DNA code.

These techniques were expensive. Only the wealthy could avail themselves of this service. With massive coercion by the media, the prevailing viewpoint became that those who were successful, either through hard work or intelligence, should have the opportunity of perpetuating their kind.

The drones were created later with the realization that people were needed — probably would always be needed — to carry out jobs the more intelligent would scorn. The lower echelon of the armed forces were the first to benefit.

This successful experiment led to a wider application of creating and employing drones for menial, boring occupations. The intelligentsia were perpetuated as the top of the social pyramid, presiding over a safe and controlled base.

Historians said there was nothing new in this arrangement. Society had always functioned in this manner. Yet it was a happier society as the drones didn't seek advancement, political power, or betterment of their status. Their mental capacities were designed to the level of competence necessary for their function. Only recently had problems arisen. Again my mind returned to the drones, those with failing intelligence, and more disturbing, those who were beginning to agitate for more control in their lives.

Even in this advanced age, old superstitions raised senseless fears in a babble of dire warnings. We'd gone too far, some said, predicting their god would hurl destructive forces upon us. The drones, they maintained, were an abomination to all that was good in creation.

When the creation of drones began, these warnings were taken seriously by many. Their opposition created lively debate and political opposition that gradually faded as living conditions improved and society's wealth increased.

With the extension of the life-span by medical science, and death only an accidental possibility, the shrill voices of doom were silenced in the glow of secure contentment. Who would argue when a life could be preserved by organ transplants from a living vegetable? Who did not appreciate that sons and daughters were no longer slaughtered as drone-manned armed forces brought civilization to barbaric parts of the world?

We had progressed spectacularly in our 10,000-year history: death all but eliminated, pollution a thing of the past, fossil fuels and thermonuclear energy no longer required.

The great breakthrough occurred with the discovery that crystals could convert hydrogen into an unlimited source of power. This enabled us to launch probes throughout the universe, some that wouldn't return for thousands of years.

This experiment was possible due to genetic engineering. Life could be extended almost indefinitely, with successive generations of Atlantians being born hundreds of light years away from earth.

We'd brought enlightenment to many areas of the world. Primitive species of Homosapiens were being taught or altered to enable them to function in a technically advancing earth society.

We'd colonized every remote land mass in our earth-sphere, as the citizens of Mu had done in theirs. At last, global peace was a reality.

CHAPTER 13

Prophesy

One segment of society refused to join the Age of Reason. These were "The Ones", as they called themselves. A hard-core remnant of the old religion, they clung tenaciously to outmoded beliefs in a Supreme Being.

The adherents, although primarily people from the lower echelons of society, were occasionally found in the ruling classes, furtively guarding their beliefs. The Ones had been the main opposition to genetic engineering. When the battle was lost, they set about trying to create laws recognizing the drones as creations of their God, claiming all drones should have the same rights under law as those who created them.

This doctrine was preposterous, for had it been adopted, instead of having a willing work force to carry out the mundane, dull or dangerous tasks that was intended for drones, we would return to the Days of Confrontation. In those dark times, class conflict spawned hatred, political differences and labor unions of militant workers.

I suspected The Ones were responsible for the actions of those drones who agitated for control in their lives. If this sedition was proved, they could receive the severest penalty possible: extermination.

The State decreed that all adults, after completing university, must marry. The thinking was logical as the burden of raising children was better borne in tandem than alone. The sometimes odious, sometimes enjoyable, tasks of raising children were better as a shared responsibility. Sex had little bearing on marriage, as it was realized its prime purpose was now physical gratification. Intercourse for producing babies became a memory of a past era. Drones were engineered for sexual gratification. These drones, comprising a lower echelon of the servant class, were notable for their attractiveness and prowess in any sexual function. These arrangements eradicated the love triangles, broken homes and tragedies of an earlier age.

This advancement was also condemned by The Ones, who claimed love in intercourse as a gift of God. Their condemnation was quashed by the scientific reasoning that intercourse was the method used by the lowest forms of life to perpetuate their form of life.

The established leader of The Ones was a man named Noah, a brilliant scientist acclaimed by his peers and the State for his pioneering work with the crystals. In fact, he had been hailed as a national hero and was given the highest honors the country could bestow.

Noah spearheaded much of the pioneering work on the drones. It was his concept that provided the impetus for the tremendous scientific advances in genetic engineering. But, suddenly, many years ago, he renounced all honors, resigned as Chairperson of the prestigious Academy of Science, and would, he said, from this day forward, do the work of God to the best of his ability. Of course, it was realized he had gone mad.

Noah was in such an exalted position that it was difficult for the government to take drastic action. Normally a dissident could be terminated or confined. Not Noah. He was too powerful, having many friends in high places, including the Senate. The government decided their best course of action was to ignore his ranting. Noah claimed he'd had a vision of God commanding him to forgo his evil ways. He immediately repented and vowed to devote his life to spreading God's word and working for God's children.

These children, Noah claimed, included all people, even the drones.

When reminded that he had helped create the drones, Noah maintained he had merely worked with the materials provided by God. Man, he claimed, could only manipulate the building blocks life provided; he couldn't create.

Noah, although denied access to the mass media, was remarkably successful in gathering a zealous band of disciples to help spread his lunacy. In spite of being small in numbers, The Ones' influence permeated all strata of society.

My servant drone, Sinta, was proof of this. Although illegal to indoctrinate drones into any type of organization, society or theology, somehow she had been reached by Noah's group. Once I saw her smiling, which was unusual as drones were expressionless as they carried out their duties. I asked Sinta why she appeared happy. Her answer startled me. "Because the Creator loves me," she said simply.

I replied that the people who had manipulated the DNA to create her drone type had forgotten she existed. She was merely a product, like the millions of consumer items flowing down assembly lines in a factory. She was not, she'd insisted; she was a living soul, a part of the Creator responsible for all life. As she spoke, it seemed to me, a spark of intelligence glowed within her eyes.

I was going to discipline her for these ridiculous statements, then return her for reprogramming, a simple procedure employed when a drone malfunctions. But I changed my mind.

I knew it was stupid and something I couldn't mention to anybody, but I liked Sinta. Perhaps it was my imagination, but she seemed to possess some attributes of humankind. My feeling was something I wouldn't and couldn't acknowledge: I felt affection for Sinta. The Senate, realizing the danger of humans mating with drones to produce a race of inferior beings that would weaken the nation, insisted that the drones, like mules, be made so they couldn't produce their kind.

Noah, still powerful, reached out to the drones with a mission that would mean ruin to the human race. He accepted the drones as equals and was determined to better their lot in life. Fortunately for an embarrassed government not knowing how to deal with this dilemma, Noah suddenly seemed to go completely insane by announcing he'd received another vision from God.

This prophetic vision concerned our civilization being swept into the sea and drowned. The entire continent, Noah claimed, would be expunged from the face of the earth.

The Senate, in its collective wisdom, initially encouraged the news media to cover this pronouncement in lavish detail. It would, they postulated, be Noah's undoing. He would lose what credibility he retained.

Noah's ridiculous pronouncement then produced a dilemma for government, for he was a great scientist, the greatest in history. And though he had stopped his scientific endeavors years before, his reputation stood like a colossus in the annals of scientific achievement.

It was debated whether his scenario of doom would plunge the nation into panic. The consensus was that it would not. His pronouncement was outrageous, too farfetched. Leading scientists pointed out that, of course, natural catastrophes occurred throughout history. Earthquakes, tidal waves, volcanic eruptions had devastated regions of the world, killing many people.

What Noah was saying was ludicrous. He was stating that God was about to eliminate all mankind because it had reached a state of evil decadence which God found to be an abomination. All humankind and all creatures residing within the earth's sphere were to be exterminated.

Noah and The Ones would be the sole survivors, Noah claimed, and they would be the curators of life in the new order. It would be their duty to preserve the genes of every living species to be reactivated in a new world. His plan for survival, said Noah, was given to him by God. He was to build a huge vessel that would safely survive the coming deluge of death from the raging seas.

Noah became the favorite subject of cartoonists, comedians and ad writers. Noah and The Ones were depicted in primitive wooden boats cresting a gigantic wave; advertisements urged people to buy before the deluge; jokes abounded. Ridicule heaped on Noah and his followers appeared to have no effect. On the highest mountain on the continent, at an elevation of 2000 meters, Noah and The Ones began constructing their vessel.

His undertaking boggled the mind of any thinking person as the logistics were staggering. A huge area of the mountain was blown out by explosives to create a flat, working area. Anti-gravity vehicles and helicopters moved the vast quantities of materials to the building site.

Buildings were erected to house the workers; power had to be generated for the large machinery; supplies and materials were stored in gigantic warehouses; food and water were transported to sustain the workers.

Although a scientist, Noah's expertise didn't include ship design. The blueprint for this vessel, Noah maintained, was imprinted into his brain by God. As the strange-looking vessel materialized, it became a tourist mecca.

Thousands of people were flown around and over the building site by opportunistic tour directors to marvel at Noah's ingenuity and determination. It was, most agreed, a monument to man's superstition, resolution and tenacity. Scorn was heaped upon Noah and his group of zealots. Scientists pointed out that if there were a calamity of the magnitude Noah was forecasting, the safest way to escape was by aircraft or space vehicle. The thought of being tossed about on a raging sea was ludicrous. Oblivious to criticism, Noah continued to build his strange boat. Some of his followers scoured the continent for cells from every living type of plant and animal from which, they claimed, they would re-create a new world.

CHAPTER 14

Faith in the Future

When the furor concerning Noah's prediction began to fade, another scientist rekindled interest. Plato was no admirer of Noah, but when questioned about the possibility of Noah's prediction, he didn't scoff.

Professor Plato was also a revered scientist whose specialty was pre-history and archaeology. He was most famous for his assertion that far older civilizations had proceeded ours. He alleged mankind extended back to the time of the dinosaurs, which he claimed, were the "dragons" of folklore. The basis for his belief were facts that most scientists disputed or ignored. Plato claimed there was irrefutable evidence that the equator of earth had changed position at least six times.

This meant that new continents had risen from the oceans while the existing ones had been covered by the oceans. The polar regions had shifted, plunging semi-tropical continents, like Atlantis, either to the bottom of the ocean, or turning them swiftly into a wilderness of ice and snow.

As proof, Plato pointed to the rocks where past magnetic forces had been in the opposite direction. This hypothesis couldn't be disputed by other scientists, being fact. What they disagreed with was his premise that mankind had lived during these violent upheavals. Plato claimed there was evidence they had indeed lived before, during and after these events. He named anomalies for which there was no scientific answer. How, for instance, did a perfectly-ground lens get into a piece of coal millions of years old?

Were there not pictures of spacecraft etched on cave walls? What about the laser gun found embedded in sediment that was at least five million years of age? Or the bullet found embedded in the skull of a Brontosaurus, a giant 80-foot monster living in the Mesozoic era of 200 to 60 million years ago?

These were valid questions, but as they didn't fit in with current scientific theory, they were ignored. Plato scoffed at Noah's insistence he'd received a message from God. God was mythology, a product of man's needs for explanation when none existed, a quaint hangover from a yesterday of ignorance, he said. Nevertheless, Plato confirmed that Noah's forecast was in the realm of possibility. Furthermore, he was sure that it had happened in the past.

"If the ice at the pole became too thick, the earth would develop a slight wobble as it has today," he stated. "In time, this could force the earth to shift on its axis so that the oceans would be hurled across existing continents.

"This would produce immense pressures on the continental plates, raising some and plunging others downward into the mantle of the planet. Continents would be inundated; others would rise from the depths. Civilizations would be expunged from the face of the globe."

His underwater explorations discovered the apparent ruins of great cities thousands of meters under the surface of the sea. This, Plato claimed, could happen to any civilization no matter how highly advanced. Over centuries, nearly all traces of civilization would be eradicated. Buildings, roads, homes, anything produced by mankind would be ground to rubble by the billions of tons of water covering them.

That, explained Plato, is why only the gigantic building blocks of ancient civilizations remain. These huge pieces of rubble lying in geometrical patterns were not an accident of nature.

Plato concluded his argument by saying that Atlantians were probably not the first, nor would we be the last, civilization on this planet. All being said, he doubted very much that our demise was imminent. He personally was far too busy enjoying life to worry. He advised his fellow citizens to do the same. Plato's theories gave us food for thought and charged the imagination of many writers. Stories abounded on the premise that our astronauts would return from their space probes to find our civilization expunged, with a new race having replaced us.

These new citizens of the world could be primitive, advanced, or somewhere between. It was interesting speculating on what our astronauts would do if they found themselves in such a situation after many years in space.

Many scientists reasoned our astronauts would find a very advanced civilization, as hundreds or thousands of earth years would have passed, compared to the relatively short time span they lived in space. Gradually the interest generated by Professor Plato faded. "Noah Madness", as it was called, retreated to the end of newscasts. The world moved serenely forward as things of greater importance filled our minds.

My memo to the Ministry of Science concerning the drones had produced results. Investigation found there had been malfunctions in genetic engineering; furthermore, it was deliberate. Again the name of Noah and The Ones came into prominence.

Some zealots had infiltrated the genetic engineering facilities to deliberately upgrade the intelligence of the drones.

Their endeavors were only partially successful. At first, instead of creating greater intelligence, they had done the opposite, resulting in drones who were failing to carry out their work assignments.

Their genetic engineering mistakes were rectified and, using improved techniques, they soon created drones with increased intelligence. These were the drones demanding political rights. After exhaustive investigation, the zealot infiltrators sabotaging the drone Engineering Program were caught, summarily tried and secretly exterminated. No word of these events reached the public at large. Noah, who was behind the scheme, escaped unscathed due to his power and influence.

Meanwhile back at home, my son's insistence overcame my reluctance. Again I found myself cruising the inner solar system. I found it more interesting than I'd thought as the enthusiasm of my youthful companions from the space club was contagious.

I had received my wife's blessing for the mission as she was spending a few days with her parents. My daughter, as usual, wouldn't miss either of us as science and her boyfriend so dominated her life. The calamitous events on the planet reported late last night were of tremendous interest. We tuned into the televiewer each hour in the spacecraft for an update.

CHAPTER 15

Ominous Signs

The first report came from Mu. A huge earthquake of 9.6 magnitude had devastated islands to the north. The casualties were enormous. Air and sea rescue units were being mobilized to assist survivors. Mu itself was bracing for a gigantic tidal wave. We looked in horror as the extent of the damage became apparent. The few survivors interviewed told of horrendous loss of life and property. The following morning newscasts centered on rescue attempts and the magnitude of damage. So far, the expected tidal wave hadn't materialized. The first newscast received in space was a rehash of news I'd seen earlier. I was ready to turn off the set when the program was interrupted by an important news flash. Another devastating quake had ripped the southern Pole. Again the quake was of unprecedented magnitude. It was so strong the recorder was unable to measure the intensity. If this were indeed true and not a malfunction of the recording equipment, nothing could have withstood the quake.

These disturbances were occurring in widely spaced geographical locations across the globe due to the interaction of continental plates. We hoped the devastation would remain localized, far removed from Atlantis, but, like Mu, our colonies were already devastated. Citizens and drones of Atlantis manned the outposts of our far-flung empire, so our full resources were being directed to their rescue. Feeling I might be needed, I suggested we should prepare for reentry into the atmosphere.

Still glued to the television monitor, my mind drifted to my stupidity a couple of days ago. What had possessed me to succumb to such irrational emotions? Sinta had asked to speak to me with such urgency I couldn't refuse her. Normally drones only reply when spoken to, but again she displayed the animation I'd witnessed when she'd related her faith in a Creator.

I led her out of earshot of the household as a citizen didn't talk to a drone unless it was to give instructions. Again I noticed the astounding fact of an intensity and intelligence shining in the blueness of her eyes.

I tried to cast away feelings of affection for Sinta. It was wrong, unhealthy and dangerous to feel this way about a drone, and forbidden by law. She looked directly into my eyes, again unusual, as drones inevitably avert a direct gaze. "Please," she implored, "take me to Master Noah. The time has arrived." What was she talking about, what lunacy was Noah involved in? How on earth had he contacted her? "What are you talking about, Sinta?" She took my hand in hers (again an action no drone was permitted) and without hesitation explained her request.

"Noah," she said, "is calling all true believers. I can hear him distinctly in my head. All The Ones now have this ability." Flabbergasted, I demanded to know if she now considered herself a member of The Ones, who, to my knowledge, were all human and certainly not drones. "Oh, yes," she replied. "It doesn't matter what your origins were or your status in life, we are all children of the Great Creator."

The conversation was farcical. I who was well-off and a reasonably important member of the hierarchy, was being swayed emotionally by the pleadings of a drone. I had an inexplicable feeling that I must do as Sinta asked: take her to Noah. Feeling utterly stupid but somehow compelled to do her bidding, I waved her into my helicopter for the short flight to Noah's construction site. My actions were tantamount to treason; I could lose everything — my standing, my position, even my life. What I was doing was sheer madness.

Return Passage

We landed near Noah's vessel and I ordered Sinta to leave. "Hurry, Sinta. You know the trouble this could cause me." "I know," she answered. "May the Great Creator bless you because you are a good man." She closed the door, waved, then was gone, running swiftly toward the large vessel.

CHAPTER 16

Cataclysm

My recollections abruptly ended as we angled into the earth's atmosphere through the flaming aura of our white-hot heat shield. The television screen became visual static as we temporarily lost contact. My son and his co-pilot checked their correct angle of descent. "Right on!" I heard my son exclaim. We began the smooth glide that would circumnavigate the globe to place us in our landing position.

"Is the TV back on, Dad?" I replied negatively for the screen was a complete blank. "Somehow we've lost contact with ground control," my son said tensely. "Switch on the backup." The co-pilot flipped some switches. "Still nothing," my son growled. "Switch on the computer. We'll just have to trust that it's programmed correctly or we're in trouble." We were only slightly concerned for the computer had the capability of landing the craft without human aid. We'd have to trust that the flight controllers had us fixed on their radarscopes to clear our landing. We knew they'd be alerted to our trouble due to our sudden loss of radio contact. Swiftly our angle of entry was modified to make the long, flat descent to our landing site. There was nothing for us to do until the final approach. Perhaps we could see something of the devastation as we passed over Mu.

"Where are we?" I heard my son yell. I understood his concern for nothing was familiar. Where Mu should have lain there was only grey ocean. We speculated that our point of entry must have been incorrect. A quick check of the navigational computer showed we were exactly on course. To starboard, a dark smudge appeared ahead of us. Seconds later we could see it clearly, an enormous reef rearing skyward from the ocean and extending for hundreds of kilometers.

"It must have been caused by the earthquake," somebody said in an awe. "But where is the continent of Mu?" A stunned silence followed. Nobody had an answer. Minutes fled as we lost altitude. Dead ahead, confirmed the computer monitor, lay Atlantis and the landing strip. Estimated touch down in 20 minutes and 53 seconds. We peered through the viewing ports into a grey world. "We should see continental Atlantis by now," said my son. We should, I agreed, but we couldn't see anything. Our altimeter swung downward. "Look!" It was more like a scream than an exclamation as all gazed in horror at the hell passing beneath us.

The sea boiled and raged, gargantuan waves marching like moving mountains, their crests lashing the tattered clouds. The roaring, seething ocean seemed to have devoured the entire world. Specks of debris soon were identifiable as the remnants of everything that would float: the battered hulks of ships, spacecraft, roofs and bodies. A churning, roaring hell of filthy water had swallowed a continent.

Fear clutched us in its numbing embrace as we realized we were doomed. Although having the capability of landing on water, we could never survive this. The raging waves reared nearly a thousand meters from trough to crest.

We realized with horror what had happened. A shifting of the earth's axis, a horrendous earthquake and resulting tidal wave had obliterated our civilization. There was nothing left. Committed to what should have been our landing approach, we hurtled through a trough of waves resembling a gigantic canyon. Although knowing we were doomed, instinct and training prevailed as my son held the nose of our craft in a landing attitude.

Return Passage

We survived the initial impact, bouncing across the water in blinding spray. The movement of flight was replaced by the violent gyrations of the boiling ocean. There was no escape; to open the hatch meant instant death. Remaining enclosed meant a slow, agonizing death as our oxygen supply depleted. Death buffeted our space vehicle, hurling it around like a stick in a whirlpool. Instead of panic, a sense of calmness prevailed. There was nothing to live for, no wife, daughter, home... not even a country. Just a world of furious water, the end of time.

Something resembling a large boat floated by our space vehicle. I couldn't identify what it was, as it was unlike anything I remembered seeing. Furthermore, it seemed intact, floating upright in the frightful turbulence of the killer ocean. Recognition suddenly flashed into mind. I knew what it was and what it contained: Noah, The Ones, Sinta and living cells of every species of the earth.

Would they attempt to save us? Noah had been right in his crazy predictions.... A violent crash coupled to the shrieking sound of fractured metal, a world of icy water... a dizzying plunge into the depths of the ocean, our shroud of death.

CHAPTER 17

Revelation

The tomb of water was dispersed by the melody of Samantha's soft voice urging me to consciousness. Her eyes projected a loving warmth of understanding. "Experiencing your lifetime in Atlantis differed greatly from your last journey as Richard Nelson."

I agreed. "Was that me? Did I really exist in a place called Atlantis? It was more like acting the role in a movie. The deep feelings I experienced as Richard Nelson in my most recent life were absent.

"I didn't feel emotion for much of the time. There were exceptions: my dealings with Sinta, my fear for my job and the realization civilization was destroyed and we were going to die."

"I understand," replied Samantha, nodding. "What feelings did you experience with Sinta?" I thought before replying, "Compassion, I believe, with perhaps a deeper feeling bordering on love...."

It wasn't easy to express, though thousands of years had elapsed. My indoctrination in Atlantis still haunted me; I thought of Sinta as a robot.

"That's accurate, Richard. You experienced love and compassion, excellent qualities to possess considering the type of civilization in which you lived. The wonderful thing is you acted with your heart and not the cold logic of your mind."

My mind filled with questions. Was that really my life? Did Atlantis actually exist? I'd never heard of it. What of the science fiction adventures of space ships, anti-gravitation vehicles, the Terminations?

The only thing resembling it were the Buck Rogers' comic books I'd read as a child.

Samantha again read my mind, as she immediately replied, "It was your life, Richard, around 50 thousand earth years ago. Atlantis and Mu were advanced civilizations scientifically. Spiritually they had descended into barbarism.

"For the hierarchy, like yourself, life was one of affluence and luxury. But how was this accomplished? On the backs of the slave population, the drones, who although genetically altered, were souls like their masters.

"It's strange how slowly we learn," she mused. "The war now raging and causing your most recent death is a battle to prevent the same thing occurring.

"Did you hear Winston Churchill when he spoke of perverted science in one of his recent speeches? He said that the Nazis were using perverted science to darken the lamp of freedom for a thousand years... and he is correct.

"The Nazi regime is embarking on many early experiments carried out in Atlantis 50 thousand years ago. Strangely, some of the same souls are involved.

"In groups people seem to advance very slowly. Individuals make tremendous progress. But for the majority of souls, it is like climbing a slippery slope. To gain one meter we have to go ten."

Samantha paused, smiled, then asked if the story of Noah had a familiar ring to it? Puzzled by her question, I racked my brain for her meaning.

It flashed into my mind with striking clarity: the Biblical story of Noah and his ark. Knowing there was no reason to speak, I posed the question mentally. Was this, in fact, where the story of Noah originated?

Samantha confirmed it did. My next question was obvious. Did Noah and all those accompanying him survive? Samantha gave me the brief details.

Noah's ship was of a revolutionary design that survived the vicious storm. Those aboard had enough provisions and fresh water to last them months, but on the thirty-ninth day they saw a smudge on the horizon.

The following day they could see a mountain and land that had been thrust up from the bed of the sea. Landing, they survived due to the great scientific knowledge of Noah and the array of equipment he had brought.

When Noah died, a year after landing, they had established a viable community to fend for itself. His death began a slow decline in their civilization.

"What became of them and Sinta?" I asked. Samantha said, "They survived and multiplied. As the new continents dried, they inhabited the land. Sinta became Noah's favorite and was at his side when he died.

"She fell in love with a human member of The Ones and Noah authorized an operation to enable her to have a child. She delivered a beautiful baby girl she named Siba. Your soul, Richard, entered the fetus just before birth."

This revelation shook my belief in Samantha's credibility.

Everything, until now, had seemed believably logical, albeit some of the concepts were new to my thinking. It seemed logical that a process of learning could be spread over many eons of time to provide different circumstances and experiences.

It answered many doubts I had entertained concerning a final judgment. For now I knew there to be a judgment, but not the irrevocable life or death sentence of Christianity.

Judgment was answering to every action of a lifetime, being shown where you succeeded and failed. And then, mercifully, being allowed to clothe your soul in a new body to continue life's journey.

Samantha now claimed I'd been female, a fact that disturbed me. Surely we didn't change sex?

My doubts angered Samantha, as a bayonet-sharp note of frustration replaced her previous softness of voice. Her eyes blazed, she spoke slowly, deliberately, every word a scalpel cutting deeply.

"You loved Sonia, you felt great affection for Sinta, didn't you?" I nodded glumly. "You loved your earthly mother, although she may have been unworthy, and you certainly had the greatest affection for Mrs. Dunne, isn't that correct?

"I feel you have a certain affection for me, too, although I'm in female form." I agreed, wondering where Samantha's logic was leading. "It seems to me that females have played a large part in your life... or lives," she said forcefully.

"Wouldn't you agree that life without women would have been an empty place? Will you concede that the continuation of bodily life without females would have been impossible? Don't you realize half the souls have to take the female role half the time?"

Samantha made sense. My last life was male-oriented by Southside School and the army. The gentleness and caring was usually provided by the loving presence of a woman.

At school there'd been Mrs. Dunne and in the army, Sonia. Women, I realized, made our existence worthwhile, softening the harshness, giving us the strength and reason for living.

"All souls contain the substance of both sexes," Samantha continued. "Certain characteristics are associated with being female — tenderness and gentleness, for instance.

"Traits like aggressiveness are more likely to be related to males. It is to the correct balance of virtues, both male and female, that we should aspire.

"Think back in history. Who are the great people possessing both the gentle, tender virtues of femininity and also the attributes of assertiveness and bravery?"

I shook my head in misery. All I could think of was Samantha's displeasure. "You should know some," she said in a gentler tone. "How about Jesus, or Gandhi?" she queried. "Or think of Buddha or Florence Nightingale."

Samantha's soul peered through gorgeous eyes, again radiating the love I had come to expect. Her unexpected anger had done its job. My feeling of male superiority faded.

"Would you be ashamed to be me, or Mrs. Dunne or Sonia, Richard?" The question filled me with shame. I understood.

CHAPTER 18

Searchlight on Truth

Questions about Atlantis remained as Samantha hadn't explained why I hadn't experienced the feelings of others. "Because," Samantha explained, "it isn't necessary.

"Atlantis is only one incarnation of the many you've experienced. It was primarily to show you the dimension of time; how human life never really changes.

"It is difficult, when earthbound, to appreciate the fact that other generations in other times had precisely the same problems to face. The scenery changes with technological advances or location. The cast of characters and the problems they encounter remain the same."

I had to agree, as my life in Atlantis, that occurred around 50 thousand years ago, contained some problems encountered as Richard Nelson.

The clarity of events were like yesterday. "Which indeed it was, in eternal time," commented Samantha in that uncanny way she had of reading what was transpiring in my mind.

My mind raced back to the megalopolitic density of Atlantis. Millions of humans and drones, what had become of them? What had become of the even larger population of Mu?

"The Creator has room for every soul, Richard. Do you have any idea of the size of an atom?" I confessed I didn't. "Well, I'm certainly not knowledgeable in scientific matters," Samantha confessed, "but there are billions of atoms in a human finger.

"These atoms are all revolving like a universe. Nothing is solid, as it appears. Our fingers are minute worlds, all adhering to a great harmonious symphony of predestined order. It resembles the metagalactic order in space. Both are the product of an infinite mind beyond our comprehension.

"Years ago so-called learned churchmen had a heated debate regarding the number of angels that could dance on the head of a pin." I laughed with Samantha as a mental picture of two black-robed clerics, red-faced and angry, debated so silly a subject.

"In retrospect, it was ridiculous," she said. "But to them it was serious business. The point in all this is that the spirit form is not limited to size or space. The spirit form, or soul, is an entity. It exists as its Creator exists, and the Creator inhabits all forms of life."

I was puzzled as she was touching on matters that I found difficult to comprehend. She sensed this, I knew, as she abruptly got off the subject.

"Where was I when we got off on this tangent? Oh, yes, I was mentioning the fact you became Sinta's daughter. You were physically attractive, having inherited your mother's blond hair and good looks.

"You managed to produce seven children — four girls and three boys — forty-nine grandchildren and over a hundred and sixteen great-grandchildren before you died."

My imagination played with these statistics for these numbers were astounding; my children plus those they'd produced numbered more than an infantry company.

I visualized them lined up as if on a parade square. I saw myself slowly moving down the ranks, scrupulously inspecting each individual.

My flight of fancy saw them simply clad in utilitarian clothing, blue-eyed, blond-haired, beautiful or handsome, depending upon their sex.

The image my mind projected was abruptly distorted by a flash of reality, a searchlight of truth. The picture changed. No longer were my descendants a picture of perfection. They feared; they fought; they loved; they died.

Sickness ravished bodies once healthy; within them, bravery, kindness and understanding grappled with feelings of cowardice, greed, hate, lust, envy and fear. In appearance, they certainly were not all handsome, beautiful, blue-eyed and blond. Some resided in bodies very black. "Does this surprise you?" Samantha asked. It did, I admitted.

My mental picture of my descendants was shattered. I had nothing against blacks, as one of my pals in the regiment was of African heritage. He was a likable, quiet sort of guy who took much ribbing.

I remember one occasion well. Our Colonel, speaking to the regiment, used the expression "free, white and twenty-one." This brought a roar of laughter. I thought it was because many of us were younger than twenty-one, but this wasn't the case. Many hands pointed toward Rolly, my black friend, who laughed with the rest.

Still, deep within, I felt a superiority to blacks who, in my limited experience, seemed to gravitate toward being porters on trains.

"Do civilians all wear grey suits, white shirts, and black ties?" asked Samantha. "Doesn't the color of women's clothing add an interesting dimension to life? Wouldn't the world be dull if all flowers were red and all houses white?"

I felt ashamed again as I learned another lesson; a person's skin was just a covering, having no bearing on the soul inside the body.

As Siba, I married the son of a black who'd sailed with Noah. His father had been an embassy employee of a colony of Atlantis, a subtropical, lush and beautiful land now encrusted with a shelf of ice thousands of meters thick, the modern day South Pole.

Scott's journey to the South Pole in the early years of this 20th century came to mind. Those last fateful days when, sick, hungry, frostbitten and defeated, Captain Scott penned those last entries in his diary.

Lieutenant Oats stumbling to his death in a futile act of sacrifice. Scott alone surviving, frozen, his fragile tent buffeted by the screaming blizzard, dreams of triumph dashed, his hope of immortality linked to the desperate words penciled into a diary that, perhaps, would remain with his frozen corpse unread, forever.

What if he'd known that beneath him there slept a civilization of warmth and sun, laughter and life, soft breezes and the scent of flowers, a civilization he may have known in another life?

If such knowledge had been firmly established in his belief structure... that each life is merely a chapter that must be completed before continuing the eternal book of life... that behind each shroud of darkness there shines the eternal light of truth of our journey to merge with God... would his death have been easier than I imagined?

"Richard, you speculate. Scott, it so happens, realizing life was over, placed his diary beside him and allowed his mind to break free of his bodily constrictions. Ambitions faded with his bodily ego.

"Truth washed over him as inevitably as an incoming tide. All was done: wealth, fame, adulation. Although he hadn't the knowledge that beneath him, under the ice, slept a past civilization, he did realize that above his canvas tomb shone a billion suns with a trillion planets.

"He realized that this wasn't the end, as his journey was eternal. A Creator was in control, and that he, Scott, was accounted for, known and loved. Material gain, position or fame, was of no more importance than one grain of sand on an endless beach."

"Do you mean that historical fame means nothing? That a president's, a great scientist's or writer's lifetime is no more important than that of a common person? That achievements become just 'grains of sand' on the beach of eternity?"

Samantha replied thoughtfully, "I didn't mean to imply that the lives we live make no difference. Of course, they do. If the life lived has been one of love for our fellow man, if we have done our best for all creatures and everything comprising the ecological system on which life depends, if we have done unto others what we'd like them to do for us... to the best of our ability, then, no matter our station or achievements, our lifetime has been worthwhile."

That information terminated the session. Samantha explained that we can only digest a certain amount of awareness in one session. Suggesting I meditate on the new knowledge to gain an expansion of my understanding, she left.

CHAPTER 19

Soul Show

Sonia was in a joyful mood, fairly bubbling over with her experiences. Tomorrow, she'd been told, newcomers would attend a group session to see a soul for the first time.

"Of course," she chuckled, "it won't be the first time really, as we've been through this routine after other earthly deaths."

The following morning Samantha led me to a cathedral-like hall. Two or three hundred people filled the rows of chairs, each sitting beside their personal guide. Major McDougal, sitting just ahead of me, winked when he saw me.

To my surprise, more than half those present wore a uniform, as I did. To my left sat a German wearing the death head insignia of the SS. Beside Major MacDougal were Russian soldiers. Behind me sat a couple of Americans, one from the 101st Airborne, the other a flyer.

A silence fell as two remarkable-looking individuals appeared on stage. Both were as magnificent in appearance as Samantha or John. One was black, the other Oriental.

"We are," said one, "guides like your own guide. We have lived on earth often, like you, and are appearing the way we looked in our last incarnations."

The female Oriental guide flashed a smile at her companion, who returned her smile before continuing. "You have a point. Perhaps we have embellished our appearance slightly."

My thoughts obliterated what the guide was saying because I'd realized that what was happening was an impossibility. My eyes scanned the rows of intense faces, Russians, Germans, Japanese, Poles... all understanding the English language.

How could this possibly be? My curiosity got the better of me and I whispered my concerns to Samantha.

"An astute observation, Richard," she commented. "But English is not being spoken." She faced me with the tremor of a smile playing with the corners of her lips. "To you it will sound like English, but other nationalities will hear it in their native tongue.

"You'll see both men and women of every race on the face of the globe represented. That man and woman over there are from Tibet. To their left you'll see a woman from Borneo. Just in front of her are a couple from the Amazon region of South America.

"The majority assembled in this hall don't know a word of English. What you are listening to, Richard, is the universal language of the spirit. In this form of communication words are completely unnecessary."

The guides on stage continued their talk exactly at the point they'd been when I'd queried Samantha. It seemed as if a pause had been injected for my benefit. But this was an impossibility. They certainly couldn't have heard my whispered questions. Was this part of the mystery Samantha had mentioned about there being no time as we knew it on earth?

The beautiful Oriental woman addressed the hushed audience. "The transition from the denser bodily state to that of the spiritual state is a dramatic one.

"You will remember your religious instruction and what you were told about life after death. Some of you were told you'd enter a golden land of milk and honey, that you'd probably be issued a harp and fly from cloud to golden cloud with your newly acquired wings. Others believed they'd enter a warrior's kingdom stocked with beautiful women, food and drink...."

As each projection of earthly beliefs was described, good-natured laughter from one or another of the groups enlivened the gathering. "Some of you were taught that you'd be returning to earth, while others were told you'd spend eternity as an angelic being. Often, the understanding of what the incarnation was taught was clouded to suit the prevailing conditions of the earthly state.

"Realize that in every religious doctrine there is a smattering of truth. That truth, no matter how it was presented to you, is this: there is a great Creator who loves everything created. Everything created has a function, no matter how remote or obscure it may be."

She paused, her eyes contacting her rapt audience. "I know exactly what is going in your minds." Her voice tinkled like distant chimes. "You're wondering what part mosquitoes or poisonous reptiles play. And why there are germs or viruses."

"Perhaps you've discovered that there are none of these things here. In the spiritual plane these things are unnecessary. Only on the earth, with its intrinsically balanced ecology, are these life forms necessary. You'll learn of these matters later, from guides more competent in these branches of science."

Her companion stepped forward. "Our job is to introduce you to your soul or spirit-being. You feel and look as you did in your earthly existence. Some of you," he chuckled, "probably look a lot better than you remember yourself looking before you left the bodily state...."

I joined in the swelling sound of agreement. I remembered the Schelde with my guts spilling into the slime. "Your appearance, the solid objects you have used since arriving, such as your residence, the chairs you are sitting on, this building, your personal guides, in fact everything, is an illusion.

"Don't misunderstand me. All the souls here are living entities, as you are. We are all clothed in the product of our imaginations, to make the transition easier for you. You'll understand why in a moment when Yinglee and I demonstrate what a spirit being is really like.

"Be calm. Don't be frightened. This is the eternal soul, the energy that journeys through space and time encased in many guises. This is us, this is you, a flickering reflection of the great Creative Force."

They stepped forward to the edge of the stage, turned to face each other with their hands intertwined, then nodded their heads in unison. Then, simply vanished.

Where the two attractive beings had stood there was nothing but pulsating light. Clearly defined was the shape of both bodies, even to their hands being intertwined.

Initially, the light appeared to be of a pulsating white color, but now, as the forms moved apart, radiant colors of gold, green and blue emanated from the region of their heads.

It was spectacular. Light radiated outward like electric sparks; then the two light-figures merged into one that greatly increased the color and intensity.

As dramatically as it began, the demonstration ended. The radiating figures became individual again, then began to fade. Something like a fog descended, dimming the display to a faint glowing ember fading away to oblivion.

The silence was profound, contrasting with the exclamations and shouts of amazed excitement which filled the hall while the light performance took place. The demonstration over, we sat in wonder, all eyes directed to the stage.

The mist-like fog became dense as it shrank in size and separated into two clouds. Each cloud began to assume the shape of a human body.

Swiftly, the transformation was complete, revealing the two guides. Both smiled and bowed to lively applause. The American behind me whistled.

Memories of childhood flooded back: magicians of long ago, the smell of canvas, hot dogs, popcorn, sawdust and sweaty bodies, the cry of the hucksters promising to reveal the secrets of the universe through the half-man, half-snake inside the tent.

Nothing compared what we'd all witnessed. Even Major McDougal was impressed. He turned around, half smiled and remarked, "I'd like to see the General Staff give an appreciation of this situation, Sergeant, wouldn't you?" I knew exactly what he meant.

Samantha and I discussed matters on our way to my residence. In due time, she said, I would become the pure energy of the spiritual realm. But there would be much to learn before this happened. The torrent of questions I directed to Samantha were answered with her usual directness.

"You've experienced evidence that there's more to an individual than just a body. In life, haven't you felt someone staring at you though your gaze was directed elsewhere?" I assured Samantha that I had.

"It was because you were aware of that person's energy field that extends outside the body," she explained. "Some individuals radiate tremendous energy fields either for good or bad. For years people who were called mystics, psychics or witches could see this energy field. Many could distinguish the colors of what they called the aura, the particular energy that is an emission of the soul itself."

A thought came to mind. "Have energy fields and auras anything to do with the pictures depicting Jesus and other religious personalities with halos around their heads?"

"Yes and no, I believe, is the best answer to that. Unless it was in a vision, none of the artists who portrayed Jesus Christ and the others you refer to actually saw them in the flesh.

"Christ, being a highly developed soul, certainly would have a most powerful energy field. Even the healers now on earth have an energy field that is often far stronger than that of the average person.

"A scientist in Russia will develop a technique that will be named after him, Kirlian photography. It will enable the energy fields of living matter to be seen. Scientists who ridiculed the mystics for claiming the existence of auras will be strangely silent."

Samantha supplied more information. "The Roman Empire didn't adopt Christianity because they were enamored by it. They incorporated it as a state religion on the hard-headed, practical grounds that it would unify the empire.

"They investigated many religions, including sun worship. Many religious historians claim that the aura surrounding the heads of Jesus and lesser saints is an adoption of part of that religion, the halo being a portrayal of the sun.

"The rulers of Rome weren't stupid. Few human endeavors lasted longer than the Roman Empire. Any opportunity to incorporate the beliefs of those under their domination was used to promote the glory of Rome and to gain favor with those they ruled. This includes the celebration dates of Christmas and Easter. But that is something we can talk about later."

CHAPTER 20

A Glimpse of the Galilean

Samantha's melodious voice lulled me to another lifetime. Each time the transition became faster. This time I entered to the blazing heat of early afternoon, hopeful my husband would return soon from his duties at the temple.

On my way to market with Thyrza we'd encountered the Galilean. Fearful, but fascinated, we dismissed the servants and listened to his blasphemy from the edge of the crowd. His gentle voice told of his return from distant countries where he'd confirmed his belief in the one true God.

He was taught by the wisest of men, he said, from the age of fourteen until he was thirty. He told of strange places and animals, some larger than a camel, with huge noses as useful as a hand, but as thick as the trunk of a tree.

Much of what he said I couldn't grasp. It was all new and different. At times I became confused with his true meaning.

The Law, he said, although the Word of God, had to be interpreted with love and mercy. For often, only God Himself could judge, as only He perceives matters completely and unerringly. He stated, if I understood him, that often mankind should not judge at all, as all mankind is sinful. "Judge not," he said, "lest you be judged."

Thyrza sniffed in my ear, "Much of what he says sounds like the claptrap of the Essenes." It did, but the Galilean seemed different from any Essene radicals I'd encountered. For he seemed calm and loving, gentle and manly, even handsome....

His message had little of the radical stupidity of the Essenes: condemning life in the flesh, claiming life was merely a journey toward a great reunion with Eternal God, denying the pleasures of life to ensure the advancement of the soul.

"And yet," I whispered, "he says the great religious prophets of India agree that much of what the Essenes claim is correct."

The startled fear in Thyrza's eyes was apparent as I pressed close to peer behind her veil. "Silence," she hissed. "To think you would say such a thing! You, Rebecca, who are married to the brightest young rabbi in the temple."

We soon departed for fear of being recognized. My mind was replaying what I'd heard, as I liked things he'd said and wished them true.

He said the soul was immortal. Fearing death, his teaching that life continued after death was appealing to me. Thyrza remarked his followers were mostly simple folk, easily fooled.

As Thyrza was my best friend, I wanted to discuss everything we'd heard with her, but again she admonished me for allowing such nonsense to linger in my mind. "Not only are you the wife of Abram, but the daughter of Zadok, a leader of the Pharisees."

My fear of death was the only blight on a happy life. Abram was kind and gentle with me and the children. My father's wealth and generosity ensured we lived better than the average rabbi's family.

Abram and I rarely discussed religion. Sometimes I doubted Abram harbored the deep religious convictions he espoused. He regarded religion, I thought, more of an absolute necessity in the preservation of the Jewish peoples than the prerequisite of a demanding God.

"Religion — and the observance of the Law — is the only thing we have," he once remarked. "Our people must be kept strong by the uniformity of our dogma and in the belief that soon our God will appear to free us from bondage."

Ignoring Thyrza's advice, I mentioned seeing the Galilean to Abram. Instead of becoming angry or dismissing the subject, he became serious and intent.

"So you and Thyrza actually heard him teach?" he asked with interest. "What did he have to say?" Briefly I recalled all I remembered.

"Did he claim to be the Son of God?" I thought hard, trying to recollect the exact words he had used when questioned by a man in the crowd. "No, he didn't put it quite like that," I replied. "He said he was the Son of Man but that God was his father.

"He also said that all people are the beloved children of God." Abram nodded. "I've heard much about the man and his sayings. His knowledge of the Law is profound but his interpretations of the Law are," he grimaced, "disturbing.

"I've thought a great deal about some of his teachings and they make sense. But I dare not express this opinion to others who claim the Galilean could destroy the nation."

I knew Abram was disturbed. That evening we'd loved one another to the point of gratification and physical tiredness. Normally he would sleep immediately, and gently I would dislodge myself from his muscular body to lie beside him. Tonight was different. He lay tense in the darkness, tossing then turning. He twisted his hair, a habit I knew meant his brain was racing. Stealthily, believing I was asleep as I pretended to be, he left our bed with only the dim illumination of the moonlight to mark his passage.

Then darkness was dispelled by the candle's flickering rays. Through slitted eyelids I tried to ascertain Abram's intention. I heard him getting the role of papyrus and placing it upon the table. He began to write, the faint scratch of the quill gradually fading as I drifted into sleep.

Chapter 21

Darkness in a New Dawn

He'd been crucified. Word spread like wildfire, everyone excitedly telling his neighbor. Jesus of Nazareth was dead, buried, finished.

Rejoicing and relief was rampant in many quarters. A threat was removed. The crucifixion had taken place high on the hillside with many witnesses. Soldiers removed the body of Jesus, giving it to his followers for burial.

The rabbinate, fearing trickery, had persuaded the Romans to mount a guard around the tomb, for they were afraid the disciples of Jesus might steal his body. Jesus had promised to return from the dead. If his tomb was found empty, it would appear he had fulfilled his prophesy.

This, the rabbinate realized, could be devastating. "So it is over, Abram? I suppose his following will disintegrate without his charismatic leadership?" His answer stunned me. "Perhaps, Rebecca, and perhaps not. There have been so many stories about Jesus's abilities."

Strange tales of supernatural feats performed by Jesus were common. But these stories were the gossip of ignorant women, I thought. All were hearsay, for none of the storytellers had been present when these alleged miracles occurred.

He'd turned water into wine during a wedding celebration. He walked on water, cured the crippled and the blind. All engrossing tales, told in low voices, whispered into friendly ears.

But when one of his miracles could have saved his life, his powers were nonexistent. For Jesus was taken like any felon, and crucified.

I asked Abram to what he alluded, concerning the abilities of Jesus. Abram stared into space before replying.

"A man named Lazarus was dead. There is no doubt about the fact. He'd been dead four days, his body wrapped for burial, lying in its grave under the weight of a huge boulder.

"The body was decaying and the stench of death assailed the nostrils of those assembled."

Abram paused, stroking his beard thoughtfully. "What I am telling you is true. Calaphas, the high priest, told us about it. He is most concerned and has ordered all the priesthood to deny this event happened."

With this explanation of authenticity, he continued the strange tale. "Lazarus was the brother of one of Jesus' friends, Mary. When Jesus visited Bethany, she cried out that if he had come sooner, he might have saved her brother.

"Jesus told the woman to stop crying for he would raise Lazarus from the dead. Martha, the other sister of Lazarus, questioned his ability to do this. She believed Lazarus could not be resurrected until the last day, which is the Law. 'How can you possibly raise Lazarus from the dead?' she challenged.

"Jesus faced Martha stating that he, Jesus, was the resurrection and those that believe in him, although appearing dead, shall live." I let out a gasp at the audacity of the man. Abram continued, "Jesus also said that all those who live and believe in him shall never die."

"What idiocy! How could people possibly believe in anything so ridiculous?" I asked. Nevertheless, I was fascinated by the story.

"There is more Rebecca, much more," replied Abram, his eyes shining. "Jesus ordered the boulder to be rolled away. Then in a loud voice he cried for Lazarus to come forth. For a moment or two nothing happened. Then, from the darkness of the tomb a figure emerged wrapped in burial cloth, its head wrapped in a napkin to keep its mouth closed in death.

"When the apparition shuffled forward into the sunlight, Jesus ordered the shrouds be removed from its body. There stood Lazarus, returned from the valley of death."

I stared at Abram. If anyone else had told me such a far-fetched tale, I should have thought him mad. But my honest, intelligent husband I couldn't doubt. "But surely, it must have been trickery?

"Perhaps it was a publicity stunt, Lazarus faking death. Maybe it was an elaborate hoax by Jesus and his followers to garner support. Or, perhaps somebody lied to Calaphas...."

Abram shook his head. "No, it happened. There is no doubt about that. It was a marvelous opportunity for us to expose this Jesus. Calaphas and the council of chief priests investigated the matter thoroughly by employing members of the laity we could implicitly trust.

"That's why the rabbinate is sworn to deny the event ever took place. Our trusted agents, highly intelligent and loyal, went to Bethany and interviewed everybody with any knowledge.

"Lazarus himself was interviewed. Everyone gave the same story. It is true. It did happen. Even those who scorn Jesus and his followers admitted, beyond any doubt, that Lazarus was returned from the dead."

My mind reeled while gazing at the serious face of my husband. Occasionally, he did tease me by telling me ridiculous stories. When we were first married and I was young and gullible, I often fell for his deceptions, to his great amusement. These days I could see through him as easily as examining stones in a shallow pool. There was no suppressed humor. Abram believed.

"What will the high priests and council do?" I asked. "For if Jesus performed such miracles, surely he was sent by God, as he claimed. He could have led us from domination and restored us to glorious nationhood."

Abram shook his head. "No, he didn't intend doing anything like that. He claimed his kingdom is not of this world."

Four days later Abram returned from the temple in a highly agitated state. He roughly told the children to keep quiet when they joyfully welcomed him. He gave me a perfunctory greeting as he pushed past me into the small alcove where he wrote.

This room was Abram's sanctum, and when he occupied it, we knew we must be quiet. He would speak to us only when he was ready. He ignored the evening meal and the children went to bed without their usual hug and kiss from their father. I was hurt and frightened, a torrent of worrisome possibilities cascading through my imagination.

I followed the children to bed but sleep eluded me. I waited tensely in the darkness until dawn began to dispel the blackness. Only then did he whisper my name from the doorway.

Slipping on my robe, I joined him, fearing what he would say. "It has happened, just as he predicted."

That was all he said, nothing else, no explanation of what he meant. "What happened? Who predicted? . . . I don't understand what you're saying, Abram."

"Jesus, the Galilean, has risen from the dead as he said he would," Abram rasped in a hoarse whisper. "All precautions have been for naught. The guards saw nothing, although they are still being interrogated by their officers."

We had endured crises before, but never had I seen Abram so upset. Even the illness that nearly took the life of our youngest daughter affected him less.

I placed my arms around his tense body, trying to calm him. "This happening, even if it were true, would have no bearing on us, surely. How can it possibly affect you and me, Abram?" His eyes, although full on my face, seemed to pass through me into a perception of his imagination. "It is a happening that will have a profound effect on all our future as a nation.

"It is something I should have realized would happen. But now it is too late, for all, especially me," he said in a bitter tone of self recrimination.

I hurried to the temple to say that Abram was sick. Although untrue, it was the only solution, as he was in no condition to carry out his rabbinical duties.

Thyrza, like the good friend she was, agreed to take the children. I also lied to her about Abram's sickness. Later I'd tell her the truth. My deceptions finished, I turned my attention to Abram.

Although still morning, I insisted Abram drink wine to calm his nerves. He must sleep. He must regain his composure. He desperately wanted to speak of the matters bothering him, but I refused to listen.

"We'll talk of Jesus and his apparent resurrection from the dead, later. Meanwhile, drink your wine." I prattled on about routine matters, and topics that bored him.

His eyes became heavy and I urged him to lie on the bed. I continued talking about every mundane topic I could think of, anything to keep his mind off the subject that seemed to have consumed him.

The wine finally worked its magic. His eyelids closed and his breathing became deep and regular. I stayed beside him until I was sure he'd fallen asleep.

Abram slept until the brilliant blue of day turned to the crimson-streaked gray of evening. Thyrza had agreed to keep the children until the following day, so we could talk freely. Over our evening meal I broached the subject of Jesus.

"I should have told you, Rebecca, but I couldn't bring myself to do so. I've been following the activities of the Galilean for the last three years.

"Calaphas assigned me the task of keeping him and the High Priests informed of the teachings and actions of Jesus. Everything he did and said was catalogued and recorded.

"A network of informers was established in all parts of the country to provide every scrap of information. Calaphas, as you know, is nobody's fool. When word of the impact Jesus was having on the common people reached him, he smelled trouble." Abram brushed a crumb from his beard and drank deeply. "At first, I believed Jesus to be a radical, a man so determined to develop a following for assuming power that he would say and do anything to achieve his goals.

"But as I compiled and studied his doctrines, heard of his love and compassion, a grudging feeling of admiration began to develop. I knew Jesus was a soul of great enlightenment."

Abram, now thoroughly engrossed in his revelations, continued. "This placed me in a very difficult position, as I was entrusted to provide the evidence to destroy the man.

"Reams of information were provided. I had to assess and catalogue it. When that was completed, my duty was to write a critique pointing out the heretical nature of his ministry.

"I soon learned that Jesus' knowledge of the Law exceeded mine. When questioned on a specific aspect of the Law, he could not only provide the correct answer, but could show why in God's eyes that Law, under certain circumstances, could be circumvented."

Abram paused, looking deep into my eyes. "You know of the great Rabbi Hillel, Rebecca? Do you remember what he said when someone challenged him to tell everything important about Judaism in the length of time a person can stand upon one foot? Hillel declared, 'That which is hurtful to thee do not to thy neighbor. This is the whole doctrine. The rest is commentary. Now go forth and learn.'

"Jesus spoke with a greater knowledge than our most famous Rabbi, I think. His approach was gentler, more understanding, deeper.

"My first conclusion was that Jesus must have been exposed to outstanding teachers in the far-off places he visited. Now I believe it to be far more than that."

My strong, brilliant Abram, who seemed to possess the strength and courage of a lion, turned into a tormented child, tears of anguish streaming from his eyes.

"I believe Jesus to be an enlightened emissary of God. A part of God, if you wish. I therefore now believe he has escaped from the void of death because of God's design.

"In his being there resides the essence of God, the eternal, the everlasting. The beginning and the end. The absolute and the truth." Abram gasped between sentences. "And I denied him. I rewrote his truths. I hadn't the courage to follow him when I realized he was The Way, the messenger of God.

"Because of me... because of Judas, who I believe was created specifically to become a traitor, as Jesus knew he would... because of the priesthood's jealousy, there is now a force far greater than our own.

"Jesus is no longer of this world. But a part of it, nevertheless, in his capacity as a mirror-image of God.

"And I played a key role in this," he sobbed. "I falsified facts that helped kill the most enlightened being of all time. I am condemned to the hell of oblivion, the burning fire of eternal damnation."

We talked far into the night as Abram poured out his anguish. The sympathy I initially felt gave way to caustic anger, as the enormity of his position clarified.

Abram, like Judas, was entwined in a predestined happening of history. He had become an instrument of events as inevitable as the sun rising in the east. My strong, kind husband was the dupe of evil forces that threatened my happiness. I must find some way of snapping him out of his path of self-destruction.

Abram had spoken of the compassion of Jesus and the Law. Was it greater than Abram's own? I remembered an incident that had occurred a few years earlier. How proud of his actions I had been.

A husband was jealous of his flirtatious wife. When she told him she was going to nurse her sick sister, his suspicions were aroused. So he gave his permission but ordered a trusted servant to follow her.

His suspicions were confirmed as his servant brought word his wife slept with another man. The husband and his brother, gathering friends, went quickly to the house were his wife lay. Entering, they found the wife in the ecstasy of copulative fulfillment.

The Law states that death is the just reward for a wanton woman, so she was dragged into the street to be stoned. Her lover was already dead, strangled by the enraged husband and his brother.

The woman cowered, screaming as the first rocks slammed into her bruised and naked flesh, just as Abram passed homeward from his temple duties.

Abram's rabbinical duty was to ensure the Law was being fulfilled and, in the eyes of Moses and the Law, the strangulation and stoning were the correct punishment.

In spite of this, Abram threw himself in front of the woman and her enraged attackers. Passionately, he screamed that he should bear the punishment of her guilt.

The vindictive husband and his helpers, stones in hand but shocked by Abram's intervention, furiously demanded to know why he acted in this way.

"Because as a Rabbi, I didn't convey God's Commandments. If I had reached this unfortunate woman, if the message of God had been impressed upon her, she probably would not have sinned.

The fault is mine. Let your stones destroy me, the one who is guilty of omission. Let this poor creature go."

Bruised and bloodied, Abram returned home, refusing to tell me what happened. Fate interceded as one of those who took part in the stoning was a friend of Thyrza's husband. It was from her I heard the story of Abram and the adulteress being set free.

I reminded Abram of his actions, and asked, "Isn't that what the Galilean would have done? And weren't you chastised when word of this reached your superiors at the temple? Surely you are walking the path Jesus decreed men follow?

"You said Jesus stated all humans sin, as you believe you did in your part of the conspiracy to discredit him. Does he not understand your sin and forgive you?" Rarely did Abram listen to me when subjects of a serious nature were discussed, for these were the problems of men. My area of knowledge encompassed the home, minor social events and our children. This time was different.

Abram grasped my words like a drowning man clutching a floating log. Quickly, I pursued my advantage.

"You say you believe Jesus is the foretold Christ of scripture, that all events were predestined and that the Galilean followed the script to ensure all prophecy would be fulfilled.

"This being so, the other characters must have been preordained to play their minor roles in support of Jesus. Judas, for instance, as you pointed out yourself.

"His role was vital. Someone had to betray Jesus so he would be persecuted, tried, found guilty and executed. Without this, the prophecy would not be fulfilled.

"These events, dear Abram, also the people who carried them out, including you, must have been controlled by the Divine Ordinance of God."

I could scarcely believe what was happening. Words tumbled from my mouth as if directed by a higher intelligence. No thought was required.

"You tell me that Jesus, although not refuting the Law, moderates it in many ways. He spoke of a loving God who was not so much interested in the observance of the Law but in the spirit of the Law.

"You say, Abram, that Jesus intimated our religion had become dogmatic to the point that love of God and one's neighbor had been forgotten. He claimed that God loves the sinners as well as the righteous."

Abram nodded, at a loss for words. I suspect having his thoughts restated by another person was a refreshing change after his months of silent debate.

"Didn't Jesus say that he was the way and that those who follow him will never die?" Abram confirmed this was correct. "Then the solution is clear. Surely all you have to do now is to ask forgiveness and follow the path that Jesus advocated." Abram sat silent for a long time, lost in thought. His eyes were closed but his fluttering eyelids belied he was in repose. With a shout that startled me he rose to his feet, his eyes wild with triumphant excitement.

"You've shown me the way, Rebecca! You are right, of course. I'm a blind fool. From the mouths of babes comes truth." He pulled me to my feet. "Not that you are a baby, but in matters of religion you have always been like a child in your simplicity. I will follow Jesus from now on."

His change in attitude was as sharp a contrast as deepest night to high noon. His jubilation was infectious, for we held one another in rapture as the blackness of despair gave way to the brightness of hope.

I thought our troubles were behind us. Instead, our road together led directly to the edge of a great abyss.

CHAPTER 22

The Convert

How could I have predicted the transformation of Abram, or the difference in our new relationship? When I suggested he follow Jesus, I thought it would be a temporary matter, that life would continue much the same.

Abram was a man consumed. Jesus filled his entire life, as it did the lives of the strange men and women who had been his disciples.

To my consternation and embarrassment, it was often my house that was chosen to be their meeting place. Always, the subject of their conversation was Jesus, as Abram plied them with questions.

It didn't bother Abram that our income was now practically nonexistent since he resigned from his priestly duties. Nor did it matter that we were being ostracized by many close friends. Matters became worse. My father, Zadok, heard of Abram's strange behavior. He was so furious he threatened to cut off all financial support.

The disciples and Jesus so dominated my life, I developed a hatred of everything they represented. Not only did they hold Abram captive, they'd relegated me to second place in his life.

At first, I found great interest in what the disciples had to say about Jesus. They claimed he had returned to them in the flesh after death, and that they had talked and touched him.

Thomas, doubtful that Jesus had returned from the dead, had been encouraged to place his fingers in the wounds to assure himself that it was his Master. Then Jesus had turned to him and said, "Thomas, because you have seen me, you have believed; blessed are those who have not seen me and yet believe."

These words controlled the remainder of Abram's life. "This is the redemption I've been waiting for. The disciples knew Jesus in person. I knew him only by reputation. On faith alone I believe."

Abram sensed my disenchantment before I mentioned it to him. I was desperately vulnerable. Everything I valued in life was being devoured by the Christians, as the followers of Jesus were now called.

My husband was a man possessed, his life entirely devoted to the task of making all men aware that Jesus was the Christ, the Messiah, the one prophesied in the Holy Writings.

Abram's vortex of zeal sucked me into a sea of helplessness that seemed without escape. I was pulled away from all I loved: my home, my friends, my social position.

Fear wrapped its freezing tentacles around my inner being as I realized we were heading for financial and social ruin. I turned to Thyrza for the help I thought would be forthcoming.

Instead of the warmth of love and understanding, I found cold rejection. I could have been a Samaritan, for she looked at me with the interest she would a fleeting shadow on the dusty road.

Most of the people I knew, particularly those of education, dismissed the claim that Jesus was the Messiah; instead, he was branded as a fake, a charlatan, who deceived those of little knowledge.

"Why," they would ask, "did Jesus choose mainly simple people to serve him?" Their answer was that the more intelligent could see through his trickery.

My resentment against those who flamed Abram's faith rose in my throat like bile. When anger spewed forth in sharp words, the disciples answered softly, fanning my fury to greater intensity.

Finding no outlet, my hatred focused on Abram, who was responsible for the situation. In desperation, I screamed at him that we were losing everything. He replied by saying material things were temporary illusions. The only thing that mattered was to believe and follow Jesus.

CHAPTER 23

Counterforce

The plan began forming in my mind, and my father agreed to help. He would arrange matters with Calaphas and the chief priests.

No harm would come to Abram. He would simply be reeducated and, by publicly admitting the errors of his ways, would, no doubt, be elevated into the hierarchy of the priesthood.

Father's enthusiasm for solving my problem produced a welcome benefit, for he would double the amount of money he provided for us. We would be reestablished and returned to a place of honorable respect in the community.

Calaphas himself outlined the strategy.

It would ensure Abram received the gentle guidance he required to reestablish himself in the priesthood.

As a loyal citizen of the state, I would report to Calaphas that Abram and the disciples are planning a coup. The High Priests are to be seized, and a ransom demanded for their release.

Abram is the instigator, I'm to say, so only he will be imprisoned. The ransom demand is that the religious hierarchy publicly acknowledge the legitimacy of Christian claims.

As Abram's motives are only those of a misguided man, Calaphas assured me his imprisonment would be pleasant, providing good food and luxuries in comfortable quarters. Once removed from the fanaticism of the Christians, Abram's reason would reassert itself, said Calaphas. Reindoctrination of the true faith would be provided by constant exposure to leading rabbis.

The plan was approved and further embellished. The children and I would visit Abram whenever we wished, as would his old friends. Constant exposure to reality over time, all agreed, would bring Abram back to his senses.

The most important point would be that Abram would never know who his accuser had been. My involvement would be kept a secret.

In a matter of days Abram would be apprehended. I was not told the exact date as my agitation might create suspicion. Alternating feelings of hope and dread made it difficult to maintain my composure.

I pictured Abram as his former self, laughing about his previous involvement with the Christians, telling me how foolish he'd been.

More often, images of despair dominated. Abram imprisoned, stubbornly defying all efforts to rehabilitate his former beliefs. Frequently, the worst scenario of any: Abram learning of my betrayal.

Days and nights passed in an agony of apprehension, tenseness and insomnia. Because I couldn't find the gentle path to sleep I would lie awake listening to Abram and the disciples talk.

I was surprised to learn they believed in the immortality of the soul and that it entered many bodies in its journey to find God. This, they said, was what Jesus was referring to when he talked of the many mansions provided by His Father.

I'd thought the Christians believed that unless a person followed Jesus his soul would die or go to a place of torment. This wasn't so.

According to their conversation, this is what Jesus meant: those who believe in Him and follow His ways to the best of their ability assure themselves of reaching Heaven.

The cycle of life and death, with its trials and tribulations, would be broken. An eternal life in God's kingdom would be the reward. The need of many existences would be unnecessary.

One day on the coast of Casarea Philippi he asked who men were saying he was. The disciples answered that some thought he was the reincarnation of Elias, Jeremias or others who had lived before him.

He didn't protest or negate these beliefs. Jesus then asked the disciples who they thought he was. Simon Peter answered, "Thou art the Christ, the son of the living God." Jesus was pleased and bestowed upon Simon Peter a blessing for his understanding.

CHAPTER 24

Countervail

Before dawn, six Roman soldiers crashed into our house, waking us from deep sleep. Gruff voices called for Abram. I slipped on my gown. As the door was kicked from its hinges, cries of alarm arose from my frightened children.

Dignified and apparently unafraid, Abram faced the officer, angrily demanding the meaning of this outrage. Two of the soldiers roughly grasped his arms.

They demanded to know if he was Abram, the son of David, married to Rebecca, daughter of Zadok. Abram quietly confirmed he was. "You are under arrest," said the officer, "for being involved in a plot to kidnap the high priests of your religion.

"I personally wish we Romans were not involved in your Jewish affairs," he remarked, not unkindly, "but it seems that you people can't handle things yourselves."

Abram was marched from the house as dawn began painting the sky and roosters greeted the morning. Had he detected my complicity? Apparently not, for he held me close, saying I shouldn't worry.

"Jesus is with me," he said with shining eyes. "Nothing can harm me." Then he was gone, the sound of feet fading into the distance.

Months of loneliness followed. The disciples, upon hearing the charges against Abram, promised to help in any way they could. They denied knowledge of a plot, saying their Christianity precluded violence.

Their love and kindness was so genuine, I was tempted to tell them the truth. I didn't and couldn't, of course. I did the only thing I could think of doing, laying all blame for Abram's detention upon them. "If you hadn't come into our lives with your Jesus, we would all be living in peace and happiness."

I awaited the results of Abram's progress. He was well cared for and provided with all the Holy Writings. Rabbis with whom he had been friendly visited him constantly, patiently trying to show scripturally the errors of his ways.

All this was in vain, Calaphas eventually admitted. Rather than being persuaded he was wrong, Abram was weakening the faith of some of his visitors by endeavouring to bring them to Christ.

Calaphas changed strategy. Night and day Abram was subjected to the haranguing of senior rabbis, mocking his Christian beliefs. He now received minimal amounts of food and little sleep.

Despite earlier promises, I hadn't been allowed to visit. Now Abram was in a weakened state when it would be an opportune time, Calaphas thought. I must implore him to change his ways, and with promises of freedom and promotion within the priesthood, Abram would surely see reason.

My father was as good as his word for again we lived in comparative luxury with sufficient money to buy anything I desired. When word spread that I had been the victim of Abram's foolishness, my friends returned. So did Thyrza, to whom I confided the plan and the part I had played.

This helped release the burden of guilt as Thyrza praised my intelligence and courage. It was what any sensible wife would do. Furthermore, it wasn't just helping myself and my children; the greatest benefit would be bestowed upon Abram as this nonsense of Jesus being the Messiah was eradicated from his mind.

Her words provided the strength I needed for my visit. Abram lay on a low couch, his ribs thrusting from his chest like ridges of sand. His beard and eyes contrasted vividly with the grayness of his withered skin. He smiled wanly as I bent over him to kiss his forehead.

This was not the man I had married, this frail bag of bones in a grotesque caricature of a person. He feebly pulled my head toward his mouth and gasped, "They will not break me nor my faith. For He is with me."

Shock, compassion and loathing flooded through me in converging currents sucking me into blackness. I awakened, as if from a nightmare, with a woman bathing my face.

The nightmarish quality lingered, the violence of vomit welling in my throat, the picture of what was once my Abram putrefying my memory, Calaphas' face floating in vile mists above me, a slap on the side of my face focusing me into reality, Calaphas speaking in low, sympathetic tones.

"Abram is like a young camel. He must be broken to understand. A clout of a whip hastens the progress where soft words fail. Not that we have used such drastic methods, for it is your husband who has refused to eat or drink.

"He demands to see those zealots of Jesus, the self-proclaimed disciples of the Messiah, the deceived ones who agitate and weaken the populace with splinter-faiths of disunity.

"I'm sure Abram is almost at the point where his determination to fight will desert him. Then his mind will be opened to the truths we must reimplant. Then your ordeal will end."

Through the unreality of the next few days, I clung to my lifeline of sanity, Calaphas' assurance: "Then your ordeal will end... Then your ordeal will end."

His words drummed repeatedly into my mind. I used them to blot out the sinister horror of what I had seen and had helped create. Guilt rushed against me like the desert wind. I tried to assuage it by remembering Thyrza's statement: "The one receiving the greatest benefit from this course of action will be Abram himself."

A seething caldron of emotions filled every waking moment, their hideous reflection casting horrors into my sleeping dreams: Abram, strong and healthy, transformed into a vile body of living death; Jesus pointing an accusing finger as his eyes burned into my soul, the disciples advancing toward me on silent feet as they carried my dead Abram, but still professing love; Abram, ripping the death shroud from his head and shouting that I was his betrayer.

It ended quietly, snuffed out like the flame of a candle. Just the smoldering wick testified where the light had been. Abram was dead. They surrounded me, held me, comforted me, those closest to me. Even Calaphas was there, for he'd brought the sad news. Abram willed it this way, Calaphas said. It had been his choice to not sustain life by eating or drinking. Before he died they had tried force-feeding him without success. Abram was a victim of this religious cult of the Christians. God would surely forgive him on Judgment Day, as his reasoning had been swept away in the flood of lies the Nazarene had preached.

I lived with my children in the gloom of loneliness, the mists of guilt cold on my heart. My father's money provided all the physical comforts; my friends rallied their support.

With their help, time played its healing role as the sunlight began to pierce the pall, and life returned. Wise voices assured me I was the victim who had done everything in her power to do what was right. I listened, eventually almost believing it was true.

I was still young and attractive. Saul, a prosperous merchant friend of Thyrza's husband, was a guest at a party to which I was invited. She'd hinted that Saul and I had a lot in common.

Saul was handsome, charming and only a few years my senior. I was immediately attracted to him. Recently, he'd lost his wife and was left alone to cope with three children. My sympathy for his plight was overshadowed by an intuitive feeling that my lonely days were at an end.

Saul and I were married in the temple by Calaphas, a great honor. Thyrza, bubbling with enthusiasm and proud as a peacock about her matchmaking, clucked over me like a mother hen. Our life together was comfortable, buttressed by our social position, our friends and our children. The love I'd felt for Abram had been greater, but Saul and I were happy.

Only in the stillness of the night and upon my deathbed as an old and honored woman did my complicity in Abram's death haunt me. My guilt swept in like a sandstorm, each needle of driven sand piercing my shell of forgetfulness with a stern message: "Is your brief happiness worth everlasting damnation?"

CHAPTER 25

The Deathless Soul

There was no eternal damnation, only the supportive love of Samantha greeting me. My guilt was deserved, I felt. I gave up by taking the easy way. "As Rebecca I cared only about myself and my personal happiness. Money, comfort and social standing were my criteria. I was also selfish, lacking courage or loyalty." The sunlight of Samantha's smile briefly punctuated her seriousness. "It's not that easy being a woman, is it?" I realized she referred to my previous chauvinistic attitude, so I grinned at her.

"Don't think you're alone in these faults," Samantha said unsmilingly, returning to the subject of my life as Rebecca. "You know the saying 'a bird in the hand is worth two in the bush'. Earthly life is having a bird in the hand. The birds in the bush are the promised afterlife. Maybe there is one; perhaps there isn't.

"The Bible states that Satan's number is 666 and people for centuries have been trying to search for that number concerning beliefs or things abhorrent to them.

"Early in the Protestant reformation, rumors were spread that this number could be clearly seen in the Pope's insignia. All sorts of equations have been produced to show that whoever the current enemy is he is the one possessing this number.

"The wise men who arrived in Bethlehem for the birth of Jesus are thought to have been astrologers. Even today, many people take the subject seriously. Do you know what the number 666 stands for in astrological charts?

"The number 666 means materialism," she said. "The money, the social position, the power to dominate, all the things that upset you when you review your life as Rebecca. Could that be the reason Satan is so often mentioned?" Palestine still clawed at my emotions. I asked Samantha about Abram. "Abram's kindness and devotion to God throughout his life elevated him to a higher plane of spiritual development.

"I'm not implying he doesn't enter the earthly plane, as advanced souls often do to help mankind. Most remain anonymous, leading lives of no historical significance, and noted by only those whose lives they touch."

"Samantha, why is it that Christianity doesn't tell the truth about reincarnation?" As she didn't reply, I continued, "Other religions, Judaism and Islam, I believe, likewise speak of only one lifetime upon which you are judged." I fell silent, my knowledge reaching its limit.

The slightest hint of a smile denied the severity of Samantha's expression. "I knew this question would arise. It always does with those brought up in the religious faiths you've mentioned.

"Although every soul experiences the same irrefutable proof of reincarnation during many lifetimes, it's difficult to convince many this is so." She spoke hesitantly, "I was guide to a fundamental Protestant preacher who could think of nothing but Heaven or Hell.

"For a very long time, if earth time had been in use here, he simply refused to believe what was happening to him. His belief structure was so firmly embedded he couldn't readjust.

"He was convinced the guides were agents of the devil. When we tried reasoning with him by showing him his past lives, he said we were angels of darkness.

"He knew Heaven was a place of golden cities and winged angels, who spent their time singing the praises of God. He didn't realize we worship God in every act of love and kindness. But to answer your important question — why reincarnation is not universally accepted — Truth in all religions is to love your God and all that is created.

"That message is too basic, too simple. Religious leaders believe they can improve the message. Sometimes this is done by sincere people who want to help their fellowmen. Unfortunately, more often, it is embellished by those in authority seeking to strengthen their positions.

"Greed, power, material gain — the same temptations experienced during your life as Rebecca — motivate their efforts. They convince themselves they are doing what is best to further their agenda, be it religious, nationalistic, or the acquisition of money and power.

"Religious leaders realize a person's earthly life is of utmost importance. And it's true we advance faster spiritually in bodily life than we do in this halfway house.

"I don't mean to say that you will not learn a great deal here; you certainly will. More, than in bodily life, but this learning will be dimmed when you again enter the earthly sphere.

"Many religious leaders came to the conclusion that if reincarnation was accepted, their followers wouldn't make the effort to become one with God. Their reasoning was people would think, 'I've got all eternity to reach God, so during this lifetime I might as well enjoy myself.'

"You see, Richard, until we can free ourselves from the limiting things of the earthly life, particularly our egos, we delude ourselves concerning the importance of material gain. Hundreds of millions of people on earth do believe in reincarnation, mainly in the Eastern countries. Millions in the Western world, as well, have always believed in its truth. Greek philosophers first expounded the theory in the west, and many early Christians most certainly accepted pre-existence of the soul. Throughout history many brilliant minds have accepted reincarnation. According to the enlightened soul Buddha, there are four modes of birth, each apparently the result of the degree of awareness achieved in previous lives. He said, 'Brethren, in this world, one comes into existence in the mother's womb without knowing, stays in it without knowing, and comes out from the mother's womb without knowing; this is the first.

"'Brethren, one comes into existence in the mother's womb knowingly, stays in it without knowing, and comes out from it without knowing; this is the second.

"'Brethren, one comes into existence in the mother's womb knowingly, stays in it knowingly, and comes out from it without knowing; this is the third.

"'Brethren, in this world, one comes into existence in the mother's womb knowingly, stays in it knowingly, and comes out from it knowingly; this is the fourth.'

"Buddha was revealing how knowledge is gradually acquired through successive lifetimes. When a soul reaches that plateau of learning he calls the fourth, his journey should be nearing its destination, for now he will understand his journey is to become one with the Creator.

"It wasn't only Christian leaders that thought they could improve upon the truth. While Christianity used hell, brimstone and fire to frighten people, the Brahmins, who believed in reincarnation, were taught that not obeying the laws promulgated by their leaders would condemn their soul to enter a lower life form at death. They could become a fly or a cow, for instance.

"Both punishments should appear ridiculous to anyone who thinks. Christians sneered at those who avoided killing anything in the belief it might contain the soul that was once a person. Likewise, those who believed in reincarnation couldn't fathom Christians worshiping a god who was portrayed as utterly cruel, a god whose judgment of a person, during one short lifetime, could condemn that person to an everlasting hell."

Samantha sighed. "I hope I'm not imparting too much information; there is so much we should know. The magnificent thing in knowing the truth is this: we can face any situation knowing we have created it.

"If a lifetime is wonderful, we can rejoice because we have earned it. If another lifetime is cruel and difficult, we can persevere in the knowledge we are being given the opportunity of correcting some fault within us."

My dubious expression was evident to Samantha, for she smiled, placing her hand on mine. "If you had a terrible toothache, you'd have gone to a dentist. Right?" I nodded.

"The dentist might drill or perhaps extract a tooth. Right?" Again I nodded.

"The last time I was in a bodily state, going to a dentist was very unpleasant," she laughed, "but the short-term pain was very worthwhile and soon forgotten."

The light of understanding flickered in my mind. "I chose to go to the dentist because I needed his services, although I knew there would be pain. Nevertheless, I went because it was the only thing to do. Is this how karma operates, Samantha?" Her eyes sparking, Samantha replied, "I must remember to use that example again, for it seems to have impressed upon you the logical simplicity and the beautiful truth of karma." I asked Samantha why we forgot previous lives when in the earthly state.

"As Buddha pointed out, Richard, more advanced souls often do not," she replied. "It might be too much of a temptation for most, who are not so spiritually advanced, if they knew the transition from bodily to soul life was so easy. Perhaps they would choose death rather than the tough lessons they have chosen to face in bodily form. This would mean they were postponing the inevitable.

"We choose our journeys with the guidance of higher souls. The particular lives we choose are the ones that should give us the experiences we need to advance spiritually." A vividly horrible memory from my last life as a soldier manifested itself. The German soldier was in agony as the fire from the flame-thrower seared deeper into his sizzling flesh. Black holes, once housing his eyes, glared blankly above the darkened gristle that recently was his nose. Lips as thick as bicycle tires muffled the dreadful screams to a muted gurgle. Major MacDougal emptied the remaining rounds in his Sten gun into that pitiful skull.

"Surely, Samantha," I asked, "if a person is in agony with cancer or some other indescribable pain, it isn't wrong for them to commit suicide, or, if they can't due to their condition, to kill them?" She nodded. "Under those circumstances, perhaps, but that wasn't what I meant. My point is a person lacks the right to end his or her life due to the circumstances in which they find themselves — unhappy marriages, cheating spouses, crippled or deformed bodies, lack of a decent job, maladjusted children, social deprivation, being in a maligned racial group, or being born a slave. These conditions must be endured as part of the karmic lesson. To end an earthly life under these circumstances would mean the lesson would be repeated."

"I understand what you are saying, Samantha. Are there further reasons reincarnation is rejected by Christianity?"

She nodded. "Again, the answer is ambiguous, I'm afraid." Her serious expression had a habit of fading in the radiance of her smile. "In early Christianity the pre-existence of souls was accepted by many, as it was by some early Jewish faiths.

"There's an important thing to remember about Christianity and the things Jesus is supposed to have said. The legends of Christianity were handed down by word of mouth for many years before being written. To this time, there are differences in Biblical accounts of events. In the early church there were many differing viewpoints and beliefs. Gnostic Christians, for instance, believed in Christ as the Redeemer, but since His function was to deliver mankind from the thralldom of the flesh, He himself was not composed of flesh. His body, they insisted, was a projection by the will of God."

This was an interesting hypothesis, as I now knew from experience the phantom or projected body to be a fact. All I needed for proof was to look at Samantha. Before further discussion, she continued.

"Plainly, this belief subverted the entire Christian doctrine of the crucifixion and the resurrection. So the greatest battle in the early church was to establish Christ was of the flesh.

"The battle raged into the second century when intellectuals blended the two beliefs in hope they were making a synthesis of the truth.

"The first Gospel, that of John, was written some sixty years after the resurrection of Jesus. This was only one of many gospels that were judged as to their authenticity. Many were disallowed because they were at variance with the eventual compromise that became truth.

"Even John's Gospel caused trouble for it differs from the others as to the death and resurrection of Jesus.

"According to John, Jesus died on the fourteenth day of the Jewish month Nisan, the day they slayed the Passover lamb. If correct, Jesus could not have lived to eat the Passover supper — the Last Supper that the other Gospels describe.

"This caused trouble in the early church because some Christians followed John's Gospel and celebrated the Crucifixion while others celebrated the Resurrection.

"The difficulties of the early Christians were many. So that you'll have an understanding of what they were, I'll briefly describe them."

I interrupted to say it was my understanding that the Bible was of Divine revelation, the Word of God. Then, how could it be wrong?

"God is never wrong, Richard. But those men who speak for God often are. Many Gospels weren't written until a century after Jesus lived. Their authenticity as the work of their alleged author is often in dispute. There is the problem of translation and understanding. As you know, there are hundreds of Christian churches all believing they are the ones who really understand what the Bible is saying.

"Christians claim the Ten Commandments contain the sentence "Thou shalt not kill." The Bible does not say this; the trouble is in translation. Both the Hebrew language of the Old Testament and the Hellenistic Greek of the New Testament have one verb that means 'to kill' and another word that is specific to the act of 'murder'. Always, in the original texts, the word meaning 'murder' is used.

"The Gospels differ. Some mention specific events while others totally ignore them. Luke makes no mention of the flight of the Jews into Egypt. Matthew says Jesus was visited by the Maji in a house, implying Joseph and Mary were living in Bethlehem. Luke says he was laid in a manger and mentions nothing about the Magi. Luke doesn't mention the supposed massacre of the children at Bethlehem; neither does the Roman historian Josephus, whose writing, in great detail, covers the reign of Herod the Great. The other Gospel writers do mention the massacre. Who is correct?

"Roman history states Herod the Great died in 4 BC. How could Jesus have been born 'in the days of Herod the King' as both Luke and Matthew claim?

"It wasn't until the year 553, during the Fifth Ecumenical Council at Constantinople, that the belief in reincarnation was officially and finally abolished by the church. This didn't end the belief of hundreds of thousands of Christians. In the 12th Century the Catholic Church launched a so-called 'holy crusade' in the south of France to wipe out thousands of Christians, called the Cathars, who believed in reincarnation. You see," Samantha said sadly, "these poor people rejected the idea of purgatory, as they knew that reaching the Creator is a matter of the transmigration of the soul through many births. What frightful things are done in the name of God."

She continued, "The Inquisition was justified by Augustine's theory that constraint may be exercised on heretics for the love of their souls. In other words, the church decreed it correct to burn at the stake those who disagreed with its doctrines. Do you know why they burned people, Richard?" I assured her I didn't. "Because the church claimed it abhorred the shedding of blood.

Augustine, by the way, used the analogy of saving the body by amputating the rotten limb. The body was then interpreted as the church, and the rotten limb, the heretic."

Samantha, her distaste evident, concluded, "I'm getting off the subject. Many of us lived in these times and, I'm ashamed to say, were party to this cruelty. Our egos, greed, and lust for power turned us into monsters." Samantha's words sent a chill through me when she said that many of us were party to the cruelty. I knew from experience she didn't imply things like that without reason. Whatever I'd done in many lives was not a secret to Samantha. As my guide, her objective was to show me the events that molded my present spiritual status. I lacked hesitation in asking, "Did I live in the times mentioned? Could I see the part I played?" Her hand caressed mine. "We won't dwell on that life too extensively, but from 1316 until your death five years later, you were a trusted advisor to Pope John XXII." Knowing I walked in the halls of power in the shadow of a high-ranking personage excited me. Samantha reminded me it hadn't been the first time, for as Rebecca I'd been exposed to the power of a man much greater.

Samantha took my hands in hers; her eyes, reaching into my soul, absorbed all energy. It is the only way I can describe what was happening. Without warning, I swirled in vortex of colors.

Then the indescribable. A million copulations in an instant. Samantha was me; I was her, infusing each other with love and deep understanding. There was no thought of sex or self gratification. It was an expression of complete, egoless love.

It ended as a lovely dream. I tried to maintain this mystical state of unconditional love, but failed as it drifted away like clouds over the horizon.

"Wow!" I exclaimed, feeling ashamed of an unimaginative expression for an experience so magnificent. "What happened between us?"

"It was a consummation of love in the spiritual sense, Richard. Even in the earth state you have felt it, I'm sure. With Sonia, no doubt, or, when separated from someone you love, feeling a mystical, telepathic bond of connection.

"It's a reflection of the glory of the Creator, a shadow of how we will feel when we are consumed in that great Creative Force of God. It has nothing to do with gender. It is the intermingling of pure love."

CHAPTER 26

Pious Potentate

The rapture of Samantha's voice floated me across the echoes of time into a forgotten reality in Avignon, France in the year 1318.

For months the problem of our financial plight filled my every waking hour. Since the Papacy had relocated in France, our monetary condition worsened and it was my responsibility to devise a plan to bolster revenues.

I reviewed events as I crossed the quadrangle leading to the Pope's palace. John XXII was an impatient, demanding man whose excesses knew no limitation. He indicated clearly he would enjoy the prestige of the papacy to its limit. The world was moving into a different era, an age that saw the power of the Holy See in decline. There were many reasons, including the rise in nationalism and sectarian movements. Until recently, our revenues seemed unlimited. With papal power supreme and nothing to oppose it, taxes on the faithful were levied at will. With dramatic suddenness, things changed. There was ferment within the principalities that formerly collected the Crusade tax for the sole benefit of the papacy. Now these revenues were employed to finance the principalities who had fought an expensive war.

England had rebelled and broken its solemn word that it would remain a fiefdom of the papacy. Its considerable contribution to our revenues was no longer being paid. I remembered the unpleasant scene of a few nights ago. His Holiness, unreasonable with too much wine, screamed that we must do something drastic to obtain money. He was Christ's Vicar on earth, he reminded us, and his will must be obeyed. We'd tried reasoning by reminding him of the experience of his predecessor, Boniface. When King Philip of France had taxed the clergy, Boniface retaliated by threatening him with excommunication. France immediately refused all shipments of gold to Rome.

Boniface, as well, had claimed his right of action on Peter's authority, stating that every person must be a subject of the Roman pontiff. Pope John, red-faced with anger, waved us to silence. He knew the story of Boniface's capture and confinement, leading to his death. "Your Holiness," I'd implored, "you must realize that new winds are sweeping across many lands. Temporal rulers are undermining our strength. The great catharsis of the crusades that unified Christendom, temporarily stemming the tide of nationalism, is over.

"We must devise other means of regaining wealth and power. I believe it is possible if we look not to kings and princes, but to the greed and fear in common men." Pope John became unusually silent, drumming his fingers impatiently on the table. He leaned forward, his eyes bright under heavy lids. "And you have a plan to accomplished this?" "I have, your Excellency." I had, indeed, the ideas spewing into my mind when sleep should have beckoned. Often, until the light of dawn, my tormented mind whirled with ideas, most fading into the mists of fatigue. Others remained to blossom in the unwelcome light of day, becoming blueprints of reality. My insomnia became chronic, the financial problems joined by another matter more unsettling. I wondered if Satan was masterminding my dilemma?

Simone was the culprit. She was my heaven and my hell, daughter of a Knight Templar, whom the king of France and the Papacy had helped destroy when their wealth and power became too strong. These Knights, who in the past had unified the church by their dedication in the Crusades, were now a thorn in our side, a product of a bygone age, irrelevant to our present cause. Simone became a nun, to the delight of her family. Soon after she'd joined the convent, I saw her.

As the convent filed by to kiss John's papal ring, a novice nun demanded my attention. Even in her black attire Simone was beautiful, moving with the grace of a queen, her face that of an angel.

I couldn't escape my memory of her. It haunted me from the first time I'd laid eyes on Simone. A great gnawing hunger filled my body, a feeling I'd reserved for God but never felt as intensely. I fought and prayed that this vision of desire would be smitten from my mind.

I was overwhelmed. I devised a plan to have her assigned to my staff. Not to arouse suspicion, I noted her usual rear position in the file of Sisters entering chapel. As I was entitled to ten more servants, having recently been elevated to Cardinal, I ordered the ten last novice Sisters to report to me for duty.

I wrestled with my desires, the gates of hell grappling with the glory of heaven. God in the Highest fought with the womanly form of Simone, the Song of Solomon entwined in mental combat with my vows of chastity. But always, the form of Simone, the thrusting form of her breasts, the magnificence of her smoldering, brown eyes, the rhythmic sway of her walk gained ascendancy.

Lying awake, fighting desires that cried out for eternal retribution, I grappled with my mind to dwell on Vatican business. But Simone always swept away my determination, her eyes closed in ecstasy as I mentally penetrated her magnificent body.

My plan was ready to present to His Holiness. It was, I thought, simple yet effective and would increase the income of the Church dramatically. The first strategy embraced the Church itself.

As in any organization, the chance to advance in rank was often the magnet that enabled people to endure the arduous days of being subservient to others, dreaming, projecting yourself forward in time to days when authority and power were in your hands and others responded unquestioningly to your orders. This was true not only in the church, but in the army, in service to a king, in any endeavor where men could obtain promotion. In the church, many dreamed of being appointed a bishop.

Being a bishop offered the first real sense of command, as a bishop had the authority to ordain priests and the prestige and power of running a diocese.

Competition for bishoprics was fierce and often involved factors other than competence. Those aspiring to become bishops frequently offered great endowments to the Church pending their promotion, if their family were wealthy. My first recommendation to His Holiness was based upon this practice. The Papacy would receive all income paid to the newly elevated bishop for one year. I knew that the lure of being a bishop would more than make up for this temporary loss of income. My second recommendation again concerned the practice of becoming a bishop. Lists of those qualified for promotion were composed by considering ability and length of service to the Church.

Still, pressure was sometimes brought to bear, usually by money, to place names on the list of those who were not qualified. Rather than have this practice used occasionally, it should be an established procedure, I recommended. The reasoning was straightforward: those who sacrifice the most to serve as bishops will, without doubt, give the most in service to the Church.

My third idea I was uneasy about, for it concerned His Holiness and his appetite for lavish entertainment whenever he visited his far-flung empire. I knew the dioceses dreaded the expenses incurred in the entertainment of Pope John and his staff. My suggestion was this: that His Holiness would be paid not to visit his dioceses.

His Holiness flew into such a violent rage when I hesitatingly presented my last idea that I feared for my position. It was only when he was calmed, and the sums of money that could be expected from this plan's implementation were expounded, that he patted me on the shoulder telling me how valuable I was. These first three ideas were directed at internal Church affairs. My fourth recommendation was the most daring and lucrative. We would again sell indulgences.

The sale of indulgences was successfully used to finance the Crusades. After much bitter debate, it was agreed that with the Pope's authority based on that given Peter, he had the right to reduce the amount of time a soul spent in purgatory.

At first, the reduction in purgatory-time could be earned by the payment of money or by serving the Pope on the field of battle, such as the Crusades. Eventually, indulgences were granted for other worthy services to the Mother Church: building of hospitals, cathedrals, and bridges, etc.

The belief in purgatory was frightening, although people were taught it was necessary to endure its hardships to enter Heaven. Only those in God's Grace had the privilege of being purified of sin in this way. All others went directly to Hell. Many in the church itself argued that indulgences were wrong. How can the church, or even the Pope himself, free a soul from his obligation to suffer the cleansing process of purification?

Had the Church the authority to grant indulgences in God's name? Again, the authority given Peter, the first Pope, was cited as the basis for justifying the practice. For, said the advocates of indulgences, wasn't the authority given Peter absolute in matters of men's souls? The grace required to lessen the soul's tribulation could be borrowed from the merits of the Saints themselves. For, it was argued, those who live a perfect life store their credits in a heavenly depository named the Thesaurus Meritorum Sanctorum, from which mankind may borrow. When some suggested that even this immense treasury of righteousness would not be enough to provide for all, the name of Jesus was invoked. Were not His merits enough to provide for every soul?

This argument effectively stayed the opposition. For, if they disagreed, they were demeaning Christ by implying His merits were inadequate. As a lowly priest, I anguished over the granting of indulgences. I soon learned to keep my counsel to myself because of the Church's readiness to brand dissenters as heretics, who found their absolution in the roaring fires of destruction.

Once I had been promoted, my earlier misgivings had been swept away by the realization of the importance of church financing by the granting of indulgences. How could God condemn His Church for raising money to do His work?

To my relief, my suggestions gained approval, but not without bitter debate by all those summoned to Avignon. However, the recommendations were quickly implemented, as the precarious financial position of the Holy See was desperate.

Within two years I could report to his Holiness that our income was now larger than that of the king of France. My star shone brightly in the halls of power. My infatuation with Simone grew stronger with every passing day. I continued to battle the passions raging within me, with little success. After all, I thought, it is what many succumb to, including Pope John.

I must have Simone or I'd go out of my mind. She dominated every thought, even when I should be concentrating on important matters. His Holiness recently remarked my head seemed lost in the clouds. It was, in clouds of desire. I decided to approach her in a very subtle way. The first problem was how to speak to her without raising suspicion. The opportunity came as if borne on the wings of angels.

I learned Simone was to be disciplined. She was overheard criticizing the Church for the way it handled young people charged with heresy. I demanded she be brought before me as the seriousness of the charge warranted my intervention. Summoned to my chambers, Simone was disdainfully entrusted to me by the head of her Order, whom I dismissed with curt thanks. I disliked this loyal, unlovely and wretched woman who, as far as I was concerned, was the epitome of hell. This haggard, mean crone, it was rumored, did far more than care for her spiritual flock. For, it was said, those of her flock who would feel the warmth of sunshine without persecution were those who would lie with her in female sodomy.

His Holiness, whenever the subject of her conduct was broached, dismissed the matter in anger. It was whispered that many years before, Mother Cecile was responsible for saving his skin when, as a Cardinal, he had been caught in a comprising situation with a young nun.

Friendship had blossomed between them, strengthening with the bonds of time and secrecy. Perhaps, I thought, I am embarking on the same dangerous road.

Simone silently kneeled before me, her eyes averted. "Look at me, girl!" I commanded. She obeyed, gazing steadily at me with those lovely eyes that haunted my nights. Something whispered to me that a sympathetic approach would produce the results I desired. I lectured her gently concerning the oaths she had taken to become a bride of Christ and the Church, Christ's body on the earthly plane. I confessed that sometimes even I entertained certain doubts in matters of doctrine and the way it was administered.

But, I continued, with God's guidance — that He surely gives His Church — it wasn't for us to be critical but to trust His way. My explanations were striking home, I saw, for Simone's exquisite face became tranquil, her eyes intense. "We should all work within the Church to contribute our best to the whole. I am, through prayer and meditation, contributing my best within my ability, and in this difficult endeavor request your help. It is difficult for the Holy See to understand how women react to our directives and, it is my belief, women are important enough to be considered. Wasn't Mary, a woman, chosen to be the Mother of God?"

Simone's eyes filled with amazement and warmth, my key to her vulnerability. "And being young and of good family, Sister Simone, I believe you are the one who can be of help. If you are willing, these charges against you will be expunged by my authority." It was easier than I has expected. Simone was completely under my spell. It would only be a matter of time until I could convince her that our relationship should extend to the confines of my bed.

Feelings of guilt were more than compensated by the warm love of this young woman. And it was love, for I dominated her every thought and molded her reason like the soft wax of a melting candle. I took great pains to assure our relationship remained secret. My staff may have had their suspicions, but never was the subject broached. The transition from a platonic to intimate relationship with Simone was relatively easy. Quoting from *The Song of Solomon*, I convinced her intimacy between those of us within the Church was a manifestation of the love of our Lord. "We are the body of Christ," I whispered, "and as such should share that love." Convinced by my sincerity, Simone became all I'd dreamed she'd be, a passionate lover and delightful companion. Months of nuptial happiness bestowed a blessing of peace and contentment into both our lives.

The feelings of guilt that sometimes assailed me became infrequent. For the first time in my life I felt true contentment. Life glided by smoothly. Even Pope John's frequent bad temper seemed not to upset me as it once had. Then, something happened. Simone was troubled. I sensed it as she refused my advances for the first time. Her eyes lacked their warmth and excitement. Her mind seemed preoccupied with matters that didn't concern me, for she refused to divulge whatever was bothering her.

Instead of the situation improving, it worsened. Simone barely spoke and when she did, it was without animation or feeling. I was alternately enraged and worried, angry and hurt.

I threatened, cajoled and pleaded that she tell me what troubled her, without success. Simone slipped into an impenetrable state, as distant as if an ocean separated us.

No longer did I summon her to my quarters, and saw her only briefly while performing her duties. Perhaps, I thought, it is for the best, for the guilt that I had almost succeeded in extinguishing flared anew. The news struck like a savage storm, screaming winds of remorse chilling my heart. Black despair shrouded me in icy clouds of numbness, visions of hell-fire raced through my tormented mind.

The hag told me, her face a mask concealing her triumph. Simone, said Mother Cecile, had been found beneath the tower wall from which she jumped, dead. "I know why she committed this unpardonable sin, as well," she lisped, her voice expressing a note of triumph. She'd never forgiven me for dismissing the charges against Simone. "Why?" I asked sadly. "Because," simpered the hag, "she was pregnant."

CHAPTER 27

Togetherness

My return from Avignon found me shaken and upset until Samantha's love enveloped me. Her understanding dispelled the self-recrimination and loathing pressing down upon me like earth on a fresh grave.

She spoke. "Who was Simone, Richard?" The answer came without thought, the picture instantaneously in mind — two women in my life combining, forming one person. "Simone is now Sonia!"

The revelation astounded and delighted me. "Am I right, Samantha?" "You are Richard. Now can you answer this: who is Sinta?"

Like negatives placed one over the other in front of a bright light, the images of the three women became one. "They are the same entity. The same person, the same soul!" I exclaimed in wonderment.

Samantha smiled with a brilliance rivaling the sun. "You're absolutely correct. We travel the road of life often with the same souls. That allows us to work out the deep problems we created with each other." Why the same souls? Surely with billions of souls in the universe it was improbable we'd again be entwined with those we'd been involved with in previous existences.

Would Samantha care to elucidate? "Let me give you a simple explanation. When we meet people socially for the first time, we use our best behavior.

"Most people can be polite and charming for short periods of time if they believe it is in their best interest.

"Is this projected image the real us? It's usually a charade, a part we play. We can play the part while our feelings are unaffected, and we can remain detached emotionally.

"It's easy to act when the way is smooth and safe. But, when we become emotionally involved, when danger, anger, lust, fear, hurt, envy or any number of other emotions come into play, the mask slips away allowing the ego to emerge.

"This is the reason we interact so often with the same souls. Being with souls we have known before allows us the opportunity of overcoming faults and rectifying our mistakes.

"If we were denied this opportunity, we would be creating new animosities, hurts, lusts, envies or hatreds that would never be resolved.

"These are emotions of the flesh, the obstacles we must learn to overcome. And unless a soul is truly advanced, it takes numerous lifetimes to master the simple lesson of religions: to love your neighbor as you do yourself."

Samantha's explanation was satisfactory, but, I asked, why can't one lifetime be sufficient? "That's something I thought you'd understand by now," she replied. "Would you really want the lessons of life to have ended with the death of Simone? Surely you would wish to make amends, wouldn't you, Richard?"

I admitted I would. The chance of a fresh relationship with that soul whose earth-plane life had embraced mine was essential. I had a great deal to rectify. A statement Samantha made earlier reemerged. Sonia, in a future reincarnation hoped to be born as a woman again and hoped to give birth to me.

I was filled with an overwhelming joy. One day, if I agreed, I'd be reunited in life with the soul who'd been Sinta, Simone and Sonia. The soul with whom I'd shared so much of life's drama.

The more I learned, the more evident it became I was only scratching the surface of knowledge. I voiced this thought to Samantha, who with enthusiasm replied, "When we realize this, we have the beginning of wisdom.

"There's an old story I'll relate, of scientists laboring up the hill of knowledge, unravelling the secrets of the universe. Each time the summit was in sight, a new summit reared in the distance. They eventually reached the final peak to find that the great mystics had preceded them."

"Will the cycle ever end, Samantha?" Modestly, she reminded me of her place in the scheme of things, as her understanding was limited until elevated to a higher plane. "If you mean, does the cycle of earthly lives end, I can answer that. Of course, they do.

"When we learn to love our Creator and all that has been created, especially our fellowman, we start a new cycle in a higher spiritual vibration."

I hadn't expressed myself clearly, for her answer hadn't embraced the things I wished to know. I tried again. "Will the planet Earth always survive?"

My science teacher once stated that if the earth's sun suddenly increased in size, as stars do when they are approaching the end of their life cycle, our earth would be engulfed by flame and all life destroyed.

He also claimed it was possible an asteroid or larger object from outer space could smash into our earth and destroy it.

Samantha acknowledged my question with a shrug. "It's apparent you'd better get into the higher vibrations quickly, so souls more competent than I can answer your questions. Science was never my strong point on earth, nor am I much better informed in this dimension.

"You must remember this: the Creator never allows His creations to be destroyed. They can change in appearance or substance; you know this, as it is a universal law. Nothing is ever destroyed."

Animatedly, she continued, "I've heard it said that the entire universe is sometimes renewed. Galaxies billions of light years apart rush away from one another into eternity, and then the force with which God controls the vastness of space comes into play.

"Gradually their speed is reduced and when this happens, they are drawn back to a central point, trillions of stars and planets rushing at light-speed toward each other.

"When eventually they come together in a cataclysmic explosion, the cycle of the universe begins again. That is the point, Richard. Everything begins anew. Nothing is destroyed."

My mind boggled, trying to grasp the immensity of her hypothesis. Perhaps humankind is only supposed to know so much. Because it is equipped with a searching mind, mankind will go on seeking, assuming it will find the ultimate answer. Perhaps it won't; maybe there isn't one.

My mind switched direction. I thought of an old dog I'd befriended while in the army. Although we were unable to keep pets in the barracks, I managed to scrounge enough food to keep him adequately fed and comfortable in a boiler room when the temperatures plunged well below zero.

Before leaving on overseas draft, I found him a good home. I loved him and that love he returned with undoubting, unquestioning, blind devotion. As he was then old and frail, he'd be now dead.

If he were, I wondered, would it be a death of nothingness, an abrupt ending of consciousness? If so, where was the fairness in creation?

Samantha read my mind by answering as soon as the question arose. She embraced me without movement, enthralling me within herself as she'd done in the spiritual plane but without the drama of lights and whirling passions. Her enthusiasm was unbridled.

"This, Richard, is within the area of my competence. I love animals and have for many lifetimes. They are souls as much as humans and the creation of God. And God loves each creation. Of course, the Creator doesn't expect the same from the animal kingdom as he does from us."

"Do animals have an awareness of God, Samantha?" "Of course. They are programmed to play their part in the fulfillment of the plan God has created."

This topic posed other questions; the theory of evolution, for instance, had us descending from a primitive cousin of the ape. Could this be correct?

Samantha answered that although everything was a creation of God, it was quite possible this was the method that was employed to bring mankind into being.

"Why is it only humans are thought to have a soul?" I inquired. "I suppose it is because we are so concerned about ourselves. Only recently has mankind begun to learn that some species of animals and mammals have high intelligence.

"Once, the criterion for judging intelligence was the apparent ability to use tools. Scientists are learning now that many animals use simple tools, like man.

"Science is also discovering such mammals as the dolphin and whales have great intelligence and have chosen to live in their water environment. When you look at the way so many of us live and die on the surface of the earth, it looks like a good choice.

"We of human form have free choice in the way we live our lives. Animals don't; instead they're endowed with instincts that govern their species.

"This isn't saying animals have no awareness of the Creator. We won't know that until such time as we can communicate with them."

Samantha waved her finger just as I was going to speak. "Richard," she said, "if a comrade in your platoon had half his brain shot away and survived, unable to speak, unable to talk, a living vegetable without awareness . . . Or, a baby is born with damage to its brain, unable to reason or think, do you think the Creator will think any less of these two because of their unfortunate circumstances?"

I replied to think so would be paramount to saying the Creator is unfair. "Well," said Samantha, "why would the Creator love those creatures of the animal kingdom any less because they lack intellect as we humans define it?"

"One of the world's religions makes a point of teaching their adherents the value of animals. Hinduism, in the symbolic worship of the cow, is trying to teach its followers that in addition to loving our fellowman, we should also love animals.

"Devout Hindus don't eat meat because of this, I suppose. Are they correct in this aspect of their faith? Should we also refrain from eating meat?"

I asked the question with my mind dwelling on the vast range lands of the West and the ranching families who earned their living raising cattle.

"Humans probably would be healthier if they ate less meat, but the animals raised to feed people may accept being part of the food cycle. For them, death isn't a terror leading to unknown horrors.

"To animals it is normal, a sleep from which they will awaken. When death is imminent, an animal simply accepts it. However, threatened with death, the animal's survival instincts come to the fore and it does everything in its power to survive.

"If animals were killed in a humane way, their fear would be minimal. But they are slaughtered barbarically, herded together so they can scarcely move, prodded up narrow chutes with the smell of death polluting the air, smashed in the head, throats cut.

"As in so many human affairs, this is a matter of learning. Although we certainly progress, we do so very slowly."

I wanted to get off the sickening subject, so thinking of the dog that had triggered it, I asked, "Do dead pets ever return to their owners during their lifetime?"

Samantha nodded. "Certainly. If an animal is loved and missed, it often returns. Many people suspect as much. A little dog or cat is killed; the person grieves. In time a new pet is found and displays many characteristics of the dead animal.

"Sometimes it's coincidence. Animals of the same species do have the same characteristics. However, frequently an animal spirit will enter the body of a young animal slated for ownership by the person who is grieving."

"How could an animal know, Samantha? How could they arrange it?" I asked enthusiastically. "The animal's spirit doesn't know, Richard, but the Creator does. It will, of course, carry over the love and affection from a previous relationship. Intense love acts like a magnet drawing spirits together.

"That is another reason we interact with the same souls in each lifetime. Perhaps it works the same way in the animal kingdom."

I thought of the wonderful things I learned. Everything seemed so logical and understandable. In earthly life, everything had been bound in mystery, no certainties, only theories or faith.

I wondered how some professed no belief in a creative force, when proof abounded. What blinded their eyes to the evidence? Was it their ego? Could they really believe that in this minute corner of the universe man stood alone, a fluke of nature?

The session ended. I returned to Sonia and we talked far into the evening. She was depressed, realizing the truth we learned would be forgotten when we next became flesh.

Her outlook brightened slightly as we remembered that in each incarnation during which we advance spiritually, the forgetfulness becomes less opaque, letting the truth shine through more brightly.

I told Samantha of Sonia's concern. Her sympathy was genuine but she said something must have slipped Sonia's mind. Many older souls, who were well on their way to completing their earthly journeys, would soon be reborn into the flesh to bring a new understanding.

The joy of this news was moderated by a sinister warning. Many other souls would be reborn whose understanding was regrettably lacking. This would produce an age of turmoil with great opposing forces of good and evil.

These times, she predicted, would produce the most enriching, rewarding, progressive and enlightened period in modern history. They also would encompass the greatest perils civilization has ever faced.

CHAPTER 28

Voyage into Slavery

Samantha said the next earthly lives revisited would show me the workings of karma. Events of one lifetime determined the situation I found myself in during the next. Opportunity would be available for me to advance spiritually if I chose.

She warned that other factors greatly influenced whether I advanced, regressed or merely stood still.

I sank into the reverie of drifting imaginations as Samantha's voice lulled me into the reality of a past life.

Terrified, we were led in chains toward the boats on the beach. These boats would transport us to the huge ship that rode at anchor in the bay.

We'd been fools to trust these hairy, white-faced men in their stinking clothing. They informed us they'd come in peace, offering us amazing gifts. Individually we'd been tricked and seized.

Their leader showed us a magical stick for hunting he called a musket. Pointing it at a shield placed in a tree, the musket gave a thunder-like crash and a hole appeared in the shield.

Each warrior would receive a musket if we cooperated by taking necessary initiation. We took him at his word, for his strange language was interpreted by a black man like us.

When the initiations were to start, the white men erected a canvas building they called a tent. Individually we would enter the tent to receive our initiation and musket.

We were ordered to place all weapons in a pile, as it was forbidden for any man owning a musket to carry a spear.

In single file behind our chief and the most honored warriors of the tribe, we slowly advanced toward the tent. As each man passed through the canvas flap into darkness, there was silence, followed by a crash.

In great anticipation and excitement, I was ushered into the darkness of the white man's tent. Without warning, my arms were pinned by two burly men and something smashed into my skull.

Groggily, as I fought to regain my senses, rags were forced into my mouth and strong arms placed iron chains around my wrists and legs.

Momentarily, I thought this part of the initiation. Then, as my eyes became accustomed to the gloom, I saw the chief and all who'd preceded me, bound and gagged on the ground.

I moved my aching head to see the entrance of the tent. Another of the tribe entered and like myself, paused in the gloom to enable his eyes to adjust to the lack of light. Like me, he didn't see the two men who grabbed him, nor the third man who smashed his head with a heavy club. After subduing all the warriors, our women and children were taken prisoner. Like cattle we were all herded into the blackness of the ship's hold.

Lying in darkness, we heard many strange sounds above us — shouted orders, the rattle of the anchor being pulled from the seabed, the groaning protest of ropes being forced over hawsers, the sea then whispering along the hull that imprisoned us, telling us plaintively we were underway.

Return Passage

We agonized over our stupidity, the metal bands of submission chaining us in helplessness. We realized our beloved homeland was slipping astern into what would be a distant memory. Gone forever was our free life, our forests and animals, and our gods who presided over them.

Twice a day a hatch was opened to permit sailors to provide us with food and water. We refused to eat the vile salted pork and biscuits for many days. The brackish water we drank from necessity.

We grew weaker, eventually being forced to swallow this swill for self-preservation. Most became violently sick.

The ship moved steadily west. The second time the hatch opened each day the black man who'd been the interpreter brought a wooden tub for defecating.

Only moments were allowed for this bodily function, supervised by two brawny sailors. For, if we defecated elsewhere, we knew, we'd all be whipped. This was no idle threat, for the white sailors slashed us with their whips for no reason.

We all sickened as the sea's gigantic waves pounded the ship. Chains attached to our wrists and legs prevented us from being hurled against the sides of the vessel. Our flesh agonized with each lunge of the ship.

Vomit clogged our throats and nostrils; sadness filled our hearts. Far astern lay our land of brilliant skies and freedom. Our bodies stank in filth, our vomited rejection of the salted pig and brackish water.

We were bound for America. A bountiful land, home to thousands of the world's oppressed who migrated there for freedom and opportunity.

This excluded us, for we were slaves, captured like animals, to be bought, sold and traded. Some were fortunate in being purchased by families gentle and kind. Most entered a hell of work, sweat and tears. Mine was such a life. Worn out, sick and old by my fortieth birthday, separated from my wife and children, I died in a dingy shack that served as home, happy to be free at last.

CHAPTER 29

Road to Power

My father, Sir Hubert Humphrey, was successful. Recently knighted for his contributions to the economy of the nation, he ran an empire of coal mines, manufacturing plants and woolen mills.

We were a family of wealth, my father having built his fortune not through family connection or inheritance, but by pulling himself from middle class oblivion to the pinnacles of power.

Despite his knighthood and wealth, there remained a gulf between us and the old establishment. We often were overlooked when invitations were made to social functions and we were generally snubbed by those who considered themselves superior.

They let us know we hadn't the breeding; we were of vulgar wealth, our only claim to distinction being the acquisition of money. Father, although a knight, wasn't a gentleman of the old school.

We couldn't point to a family tree in Burke's Peerage to prove the Humphreys had served their country, nor could we use the oldboy network of schools like Eton and Harrow.

There was no link with revered regiments, the Royal Navy or Oxford or Cambridge. My father remarked over dinner one evening, "Our acceptance by those bloody snobs will take time."

Father worked me harder than any employee. Starting on the bottom rung of each enterprise, in the most menial of positions, I wasn't allowed to proceed up the ladder of promotion until I had mastered knowledge of everything.

This was without precedent, for to my knowledge, no other aspiring manager or owner's son underwent such preparation. It was Father's philosophy I should have a good working knowledge of every phase of a business I would one day control.

My father insisted my identity should remain secret, the only exception being those who hired, such as the operation's managers. The workmen, the foreman, the shift boss, all thought me one of their kind.

"It's fortunate indeed," Father said, "that you haven't picked up a hoity-toity accent in public school that would be a dead giveaway that you were other than a working bloke."

My subterfuge was so complete that not only did I do the tasks of a worker, but lived like one with the same appalling pay, long hours and wretched living conditions.

Life was made tolerable in my knowledge that each phase lasted only until I became well-versed in its operation. This accomplished, I received a brief holiday in the congenial confines of my father's home, giving me time to reflect on the masquerade which would one day end in triumph.

Father thought the average worker a lazy dullard needing supervision in every task. His philosophy of success was to reward management, down to the foremen. The remainder of his work force were as namelessly remote as the machines they worked.

His method worked; the Humphrey enterprises were the most successful in Great Britain. These were the early days of the Industrial Revolution when, abandoning the land, the lower classes flocked to cities like Manchester.

Instead of the rich life they believed awaited them, theirs was a bleak day to day existence as the factories or coal mines consumed their strength. Their only respite lay in their drab, crowded homes and bottles of gin.

Due to my father's indoctrination as to the lack of worth of the workers, I shielded myself from any emotional involvement. Eventually, constant exposure to them as individuals, sharing their oppressive regime and squalor, opened my eyes. They were men, like me.

They felt and hurt; they could express love or sorrow, and furthermore, some were of great intelligence. This last observation came as a complete shock.

Most jobs were of a mind-numbing, repetitive nature, serving the rattling machinery powered by hissing steam. Usually, only a few weeks were necessary to grasp the essentials of most jobs.

In the cotton mills, women performed many duties better than men due to the dexterity of their fingers. So, in the mills I learned the mechanical trades that kept the machinery running.

I moved a lot. Father's business ventures covered much of northern England, so I could escape the curiosity evoked in my fellow workers by my sudden appearance and departures.

I moved from town to town under my alias, Tom Brown. The knowledge that these menial jobs were training me for my future was sufficient, at first, to nullify the seeds of anger and disgust being sown within me.

I wondered why it hadn't occurred to Father that my feelings might change as I experienced the dismal existence of the working person. Their lot in life was little better than a slave. And slavery had been abolished two years before by Parliament in 1808.

During one welcome break between factories, I broached the subject of the conditions endured by workers. I did it in a casual, controlled way, as I was aware of Father's views on those laboring for him. I also puzzled over his differing attitudes, as our household servants, from butler to scullery maid, were well-treated.

Even this low-key approach of mine struck a nerve. Immediately, Father acquired the sharp tone indicating he was angry. "There are forces at work of which you know nothing, my boy," he said. "There are conspirators who would have the workers running the business, setting their hours of work and rates of pay.

"If it weren't for the Combination Acts of 1799 and 1800 that make it illegal to form trade unions, we would now be dictated to by those conniving, evil men seeking power on the backs of the masses."

The vehemence he displayed indicated further discussions were futile. I didn't inform him, as I'd intended, there was furtive talk of forming a trade union in the factory. Twice I'd been approached to attend a meeting after work.

Marjorie and Stella entered my life during this period. I fell in love with both. The contrast couldn't have been greater. Marjorie was well-bred, the daughter of a successful barrister and granddaughter of a famous High Court Judge. She was tall for a woman, with aquiline features and gentle eyes.

Stella's spirit bounced through life hardly contained by her short, well-endowed body, her dark eyes flashing with intelligence. Her father, a supervisor of mills, had worked his way to his present position by his mechanical genius.

In Marjorie I found the ideal of aristocratic breeding wrapped in a striking appearance. As I began to know her better, I found that within the sweet gentleness of her nature there resided a steel-hard core.

Stella wasn't beautiful in the classic sense. Captivatingly pretty better describes her, with her black hair worn short, curling over a broad forehead.

Small, perfect teeth were framed by sensuous lips and delicate features, but it was Stella's eyes I found captivating. They were full of fire, intense and intelligent, assuming the softness of velvet, the sparkle of water-reflected sunlight, the passion of a zealot.

Marjorie's father administered the numerous legal entanglements of the Humphrey business empire. During their mutually lucrative relationship, my father and he became fast friends. Father cherished the friendship for it was free of the subtle snobbery usually discernible.

My interest in Marjorie received the enthusiastic support of my father. My relationship, and first encounter with Stella, was very different.

My father knew Frank Starnes, Stella's father, in an employer-employee affiliation. Frank Starnes was the brains behind the new machinery powering twice the number of looms previously possible.

Transferred to my father's coal mines, he applied his genius to the transportation of coal by a steam-powered locomotive, running on wooden rails. Although not entirely successful at first, my father believed this innovation would be the wave of the future. In a few years he was proved correct.

Returning wearily from work to my temporary hovel, I walked down a narrow, darkened street. The only illumination was a gas lamp augmented by a slash of light from the open door of a pub. Raucous laughter, punctuated by loud voices and snatches of raunchy songs, flowed over the cobblestones to be silenced by the grimy facades of buildings.

Through the revelry I heard the faint cry of a woman further down the street. Quickening my pace, I tried to pierce the shadowy gloom beyond the lamplight. Again I heard the sound, more distinctly.

Breaking into a run, I could see people in some altercation. I stopped to avoid any involvement in a drunken brawl.

Cautiously, I approached the fracas to determine the exact nature of the trouble. I could clearly see it involved three people, two men and a small woman. The men were trying to subdue the woman who fought back tenaciously.

My heartbeat quickened with anger as the large men wrestled the woman to her knees. Rushing forward, I grabbed the larger of the men around the neck, throwing him to the ground.

His companion lunged at me with ham-sized fists. Ducking, I brought my knee upward into his groin. With a roar of agony, he crumpled to the street.

The large man regained his feet, rushing at me like a speeding stagecoach. I could smell his putrid, gin-laced breath. Jumping to one side, I stuck out a rigid leg. His momentum sent him crashing across the cobblestones, his head crashing into the base of a building. He lay still.

"Quick!" I yelled to the woman. "Let's get away from here before they recover."

The woman wasn't a prostitute as I had at first suspected, for she was articulate and soft-spoken. My curiosity concerning her being in this unsavory neighborhood was quickly satisfied. She belonged to a Methodist church group providing Christian charity. Could I think of people more in need than the ones who lived here?

She'd been doing this work for nearly a year and this was the first time she'd encountered difficulty. She pointed to a small metal broach shaped like a fish, pinned to her coat. "People know this symbol. It's worn by the members of the Charity Brigade of the church."

The Charity Brigade usually travelled in two's, for safety's sake. Tonight, her designated companion was ill, so she had carried on the Lord's Work by herself.

I commented that if I hadn't come along when I did, she may have been doing the Lord's Work a lot closer to Him than she wished to be. Stella laughed. "I know what you mean, but the Lord is everywhere, even here in dreary old Manchester."

I worked hard to cram everything I'd learned into my memory as I wanted a thorough understanding of the operation of the Humphrey empire.

I'd finished with my apprenticeship and now worked in the halls of power with my father. This was the most difficult assignment yet.

He drove me unmercifully, giving me complex problems he expected me to quickly solve. This included possible expansion or upgrading of plants and the thorny issue of obtaining greater production.

I worked longer hours than any employee, often having only the briefest time to sleep. However, no longer having a false identity and again living in the luxury of the family home made it worthwhile. I also received a handsome salary.

Best of all was the feeling of competence. I could talk knowledgeably about production problems and the unrest moving like a camouflaged snake through the human jungle of the work force. Only a surly attitude marked its presence for others in management. I understood why it existed but had made what I thought was a wise decision.

I realized urging Father to better the workers' lot was futile. If I did so, it would ruin any chance of my assuming directorship of the companies. Father's attitude was set in concrete.

I bided my time, knowing one day soon I would be in a position to initiate a program of reform. Father was no spring chicken, as the expression goes. I was born to his second wife when he was in his mid-forties.

He was approaching his seventieth birthday and although robust, suffered from gout, and impaired hearing. This was a nuisance as all conversation had to be shouted in his ear.

This condition, I reasoned, was discernibly lessening his interest in his work, and possibly was the reason he was so intent upon my assuming the reigns of leadership.

Marjorie and I were a good match. Our interests were compatible: a passion for fine horse flesh, walks in the countryside, grouse and pheasant shooting. Although not officially engaged, we doubted my request for her hand would be turned down. There was only one fly in the ointment as far as I was concerned: Stella.

Stella remained in my heart. The frightening night we'd met, I accompanied her to her modest home to be introduced as Tom Brown. Simply, without heroics, she related my part in her rescue.

I'd recognized Mr. Starnes by name, his mechanical skills frequently having been discussed by my father. Posing as a working man, I couldn't acknowledge the fact, yet I was impressed by his quiet dignity and obvious intelligence.

Stella's mother radiated the warmth of her daughter. Her minister father, insisting she become educated, taught her everything he knew and augmented this with the talents of others.

He had succeeded, for Mrs. Starnes possessed knowledge vastly superior to most women in the upper reaches of society. This knowledge was relayed to Stella.

Apart from her intelligence, Stella possessed a magical allure that enveloped me in a web of emotion I couldn't escape. Time spent with Marjorie was often interrupted by graphic mental pictures of Stella: her lilting laughter, dark, intelligent eyes smoldering with passion, her pert and shapely figure, the soft lilt of her speech.

CHAPTER 30

Power Grasped

My imagination frequently drifted to the future... when I controlled the business. I tried to suppress it, feeling disloyal to my father.

When my daydream came true, it arrived on the winds of sadness. Without warning, Father was dead. I arrived home from Wiggan, where I had inspected a factory, to find a black wreath on the door. Higgins, the butler, somberly extended the regrets of all the servants for my grievous loss. Father had collapsed as he entered his carriage to go to the office.

I had anticipated this day for a long time: the day when I would assume control over the Humphrey estate and the vast financial empire it controlled. In my imagination it was always a day of gaiety. Father making a speech, tables covered with food and drink, the executives applauding and showering me with pledges of loyalty. Always beside me was my father, that tower of wisdom and strength.

Instead, he lay forever silent in the grand ballroom. Tomorrow, on shuffling feet, his acquaintances would indicate their solemn respect and then accompany the black-plumed horses pulling his hearse to the grave.

I wondered if any of the workers doffing their caps as Father passed by would care about his death. I doubted it.

My transition to top man went smoothly. The thorough grounding I'd received in the total operation paid dividends. I blessed Father for his wisdom.

My primary concern was ensuring the Humphrey empire maintained the same strong leadership it had under my father's stewardship. Yet, my ambitions went far beyond a maintenance policy as I was determined to increase both the size and profitability of the company.

Within a year, Marjorie and I were married and resided in Haddon Hall. My mother moved to a refurbished coach house on the property, accompanied by a cook, two maids, a butler and coachman. Life was pure pleasure, although I worked extremely long hours. We held lavish parties, attracting the highest echelon of society, thanks largely to Marjorie's social standing. I remembered my father's prophetic words that acceptance would "take time."

Less than six months after our wedding, Marjorie announced our family would be expanding. Eighteen months after the birth of our daughter Elizabeth, we were again blessed, this time with a son.

Business flourished. We opened new modern plants; the coal mining operations were expanded. With the help of Marjorie's father, large ordnance contracts were obtained for the Army and Royal Navy as we undercut all bidders.

By this strategy of cutting our profit margin to the bone, we let His Majesty's government know of our patriotism. The low costs signaled our approval of the great victories over the French at both Trafalgar and Waterloo. Marjorie's father wisely counseled this strategic ploy, because when parliament recommended subjects for the Honors List, surely an industrialist placing country before profit would be well rewarded.

Outwardly I laughed at his reasoning; deep within me I felt desire. In my imagination I pictured myself bowing deeply to His Majesty as he bestowed upon me a title of the realm.

Success was blighted by a shadow cast by my own choosing, one I couldn't dispel: Stella. Although referring to Stella as a shadow, I only mean to express the guilt and sense of foreboding produced by my liaison with her. Stella remained the most radiant part of my life.

As Tom Brown, I accepted the gratitude of Stella and her family. In a short time, I became enthralled with Stella, whose beauty and intelligence was superior to any woman I knew. I admitted that Marjorie, as lovely and desirable as she was, didn't compare.

My life became not only the charade of being a working man, it became an emotional one as well. Turmoil raged within me as my heart battled my intellect. Stella I loved desperately; Marjorie I loved gently.

Stella was an unobtainable dream because of my position. Marjorie was the key to social standing and success. The duel within me raged; the deck was stacked in Marjorie's favor.

I continued seeing Stella after resuming my true identity. This necessitated telling her the truth that, I feared, might terminate our relationship.

Incredulous and wide-eyed, Stella eventually accepted my confession as authentic. Throwing herself into my arms, she enthusiastically cried we could now better the lives of the working people.

Bettering the lives of the workers had been a common objective. We'd spoken of trade unions and the difficulties in trying to organize the workers. Stella spoke loathingly of the Combination Acts that she called manifestations of the greed of the rich and powerful, an opinion I then shared. Tears misted her eyes as she spoke of young children working for twelve or more solid hours under harsh conditions, young boys deep in the bowels of the earth, pushing heavy carts of coal through dusty, blackened tunnels, deprived of sunlight except on the longest days of summer when, filthy and weary, they returned to their squalid homes. "It's cruel and unjust," she complained bitterly.

I explained my father's feelings and my strategy of biding my time until I was in a position of power. Stella, although impatient for change, understood, concurring with my strategy of doing nothing until the time was ripe.

With Father's death, Stella's impatience for change increased perceptibly as she thought me in a position to act. Patiently I explained I must first prove myself capable of managing the powerful business conglomerate. Although President and Chairman of the Board of Humphrey Enterprises, there were powerful forces who could harm me if I failed. Father's will contained a proviso establishing a watchdog committee who could assume full control of the company, if I proved incompetent: my Board of Directors.

Stella found this difficult to understand. How could a father place his son in such a position? I explained, as best I could, Father's provision was prudent and wise. For if I failed, I would remain the beneficiary.

His proviso meant others more competent than I would run the business on my behalf. My father's greatest love, I explained, wasn't for my mother or me; it was for the Humphrey business, the child he'd created.

This always had taken precedence over me, anybody, or anything during his lifetime. Even in death, he assured himself it would continue to flourish.

As time passed in exciting expansion and increased revenues, it was if his spirit guided me. My greatest love, I realized, wasn't Stella or Marjorie, but the Humphrey success.

My marriage to Marjorie was a shattering blow to Stella. With eyes brimming with tears and her voice as cold as the North Sea, she said our relationship was now terminated.

I had expected her reaction to be unpleasant and had steeled myself to accept her anger. Yet weighing the alternatives, I knew it was the only way to proceed.

Marjorie was the linchpin of our social success, while Stella could contribute nothing. She was doomed by birth, poor girl, to remain in her lower middle class status.

I departed Stella's life with a heavy heart. As weeks turned to months, there was no lessening of the loss I felt. Stella was entwined in my deepest emotions; a part of me had been torn away. Just as the cobwebs of a dream faded at dawn, an idea was born. If I played my hand skillfully, I could obtain both worlds, that one provided by Marjorie with its security and success, and that world of Stella, unfulfilled ecstasy. I envied those living where polygamy was accepted.

The idea persisted although I fought it hard, burying it under loads of work, casting it aside in the whirl of socializing. I rationalized it would be ludicrous to risk everything for the sake of a woman.

The more I fought, the stronger my obsession grew, thrusting its roots deep into the soil of inevitable fulfillment.

CHAPTER 31

The Baited Trap

My meeting with Stella had been covertly arranged by a trusted servant. I'd written a note saying it was imperative we meet; would she join me at a discretely situated inn? A hansom cab would provide transportation. She could tell her parents her business was on behalf of the Charity Brigade, I suggested.

Stella neither accepted nor refused my offer. She acknowledged my note saying she might come, but would have to dwell on the matter. I paced nervously across the floor of the room I'd rented as the appointed time approached.

Twice the sound of hooves and the rattle of wheels on the cobblestone had brought me to the window. Each time the vehicle had disappeared into the evening shadows.

My pulse raced as another cab clattered down the road. This time there was the clear sound of the cabbie's command to his horse to stop. "This be the place, Miss."

Shoes echoed across the pavement, a door slammed; with rising anticipation I heard footsteps approach the room. I'd imagined this meeting a thousand times. I'd tried to envision what she'd say, how she'd act. Now she coolly faced me, no smile, no embrace. Her dark, smoldering eyes stared deep into mine. Her one word greeting demanded an explanation, "Well?"

My words tumbled from my mouth in an emotional torrent of pleading. It wasn't spontaneous, as I'd rehearsed what I was saying often. It was an offer that would be difficult for Stella to refuse.

Stella need never work again. Her every need would be provided: a comfortable home, servants, all the money she required and no restrictions on her time or activities. In return, I asked for the opportunity of seeing her when I could.

There were more benefits to entice her: money to expand the work of the Charity Brigade, a guarantee her father would be retired with a handsome pension, my assurance she'd help me plan better working conditions for the employees.

Stella made no comment as I spoke, gazing at me steadily under long, curled lashes. The only indication of any emotion was the heightened coloring in her cheeks. Only when I stopped, did she speak.

"Why do you want to do this? You're married. You have children now, I'm told. Why would you wish to spend so much money just to see me occasionally?"

I could only speak the truth that now sounded ridiculous. "Because I love you more than any other woman, more than Marjorie, more than anything. If circumstances had been different, I would have had no hesitation in asking you to marry me. You realize there was too much at stake. My father would never have consented to our marriage. If I'd defied him, I would have been cast adrift without a penny...."

Stella remained still, with tears now glistening in her eyes. After uncomfortable moments of silence, she asked, "Do you mean what you say, that you love me more than anybody or anything?"

I assured her it was true, for I loved her more than anyone else. But I lied when I said I loved her more than anything. My business came first.

Stella said she must leave as she'd told her father she wouldn't be late. Her mother, I learned, had died a year ago. Unlike my imagery, Stella hadn't rushed into my arms.

As she waited for her cab, she asked a question that filled me with jealousy. The intensity of my emotion surprised me. Recently she'd been seeing a young man of whom she was very fond. Would I have any objection if she continued?

I forced a smile, "Of course not, Stella. You'll be allowed your freedom." She'd asked for a week to think. Her father's permission would be sought, although he was fairly pragmatic in matters of her welfare.

Frank Starnes was not deeply religious or conventional, his work occupying all his waking hours. I was, therefore, not surprised to receive a note from Stella saying she accepted my offer and would be available when arrangements were made.

A surge of anticipation, tempered by a thin, cold river of fear, filled me as I prepared the arrangements for Stella's home. I'd found the ideal place, a comfortable house located on a small country estate, bought for a song due to the economic difficulties of its owner.

My greatest difficulty was finding servants that must, by necessity, be loyal and discrete. My visits to Stella would be in the guise of a half brother, a Mr. Starnes, and would explain my frequent visits. This would be vital if Stella had intentions of seeing other men.

Stella's liaisons with other men would most certainly be of a temporary nature. Although entering our arrangement like a bird in the wild, free to fly where she wished, I was determined it wouldn't be permitted to last.

This home and the lifestyle she would soon relish would fast become her cage. She would become a canary, dependent upon me for her survival. Other arrangements were easily made. The money being expended was of little consequence. Marjorie knew nothing of our financial affairs and the expense was a drop in the bucket.

Time spent with Stella would not be a problem. I travelled frequently on business and Marjorie never questioned such matters.

By this time, I'd been handsomely rewarded by His Majesty and a grateful government for the generous help of the Humphrey enterprises in providing military ordnance so inexpensively.

I was now a Lord of the Realm to the delight of Marjorie and her father, who remarked, "You and my daughter are one of the most privileged and successful families in England."

CHAPTER 32

The Trap is Sprung

I brought one of Stella's servants into my confidence — Mr. Hull, the butler, an intelligent and reliable man who directed the servants. Hull was flattered by my faith in him and delighted by the promise of a generous bonus to augment his salary. He vowed solemnly to report any extracurricular activities of his mistress.

Becoming a lady of means suddenly is a difficult transition, but a task I was sure Stella would master. The enormous gulf separating the classes was a formidable obstacle.

Stella's lower middle class stature was due to her father's genius. She was, nevertheless, a product of the working class. Her father's entire home could easily be placed in the dining room. The luxuries her new home provided were almost unimaginable. That all menial duties would be done by servants was difficult for Stella to comprehend.

Although I had gently lectured her on the fact that familiarity with servants was to be avoided, she greeted them as friends as they stiffly awaited her arrival in the foyer.

I stayed with Stella the first three days she occupied her new home. As far as Marjorie was concerned, I was on one of my frequent trips of inspection.

Stella's unequivocal enthusiasm for her new home, which had been known as "The Grange" for over a century, was evident. She was like a child, eyes sparkling with delight, giving exclamations of joy as she dashed from room to room.

Sharing the same roof with Stella was like an aphrodisiac, although my passions were kept in control until the time was ripe. My main concern was easing Stella into a way of life from which she couldn't escape. Any desire to return to her former existence would become unthinkable.

This was not simple. Stella was an alert, intelligent and active woman. Her social conscience was highly developed and she carried within her a devout and deep love of her fellow man.

I was sure under my tutelage, and aided by the luxuries that now surrounded her, her ardor for caring for others would be dampened.

At first there seemed to be little progress. She still talked incessantly about the condition of the working poor. I skirted the subject carefully, as my attitude had changed.

No longer did I feel sorry for their condition. If they had their way, I was now convinced, it would bring ruination to my business.

However, I wasn't beyond caring and had made enlightened changes in my enterprises. Children under fourteen were now only required to work for nine hours. I'd established a workers' committee in each factory or mine that met with management to air complaints.

I discovered that smelling trouble before it began and identifying the ringleaders would prevent serious problems down the road. These innovations I spelled out to Stella, who soon realized that abrupt change could be disastrous.

Most of the money the workers earned was spent in the gin mills. What did she think would happen if they had more money to spend? There would be anarchy, with a sodden work force demanding ever greater rewards for less work.

I introduced Stella to good food and wine. I scolded her for being too involved in the activities of running the house. "You are a lady now, and I want you to act like one. Sleep until noon, if you wish. The only time you must be lively and beautiful is when I'm here."

Without neglecting my work, I could spend two nights at The Grange each week. My desire for Stella grew stronger with each visit. On the third week the opportunity I'd waited for arrived.

We'd finished an excellent dinner, made more delightful by much wine. Stella, who before moving to The Grange was a teetotaler, became alternately giggling and affectionate. Pouting, she complained that although I was with her frequently, I never seemed to notice she was an attractive young woman.

Her passion when I took her in my arms was wildly unbridled. She consumed me with fury, leaving me limp. It was her first experience, she confided, but one that she intended to pursue as often as I was willing.

My beautiful Stella not only lived up to my expectations, but had surpassed them in every detail.

A year rushed by on my parallel but distinct roads of life. The Humphrey enterprises, Marjorie and the children prospered. Our name was revered in the halls of power; life unfolded in a brilliance of accomplishments.

Stella, no longer the eager disciple of the underprivileged, became what I'd wished for — a thoroughly competent mistress whose lavish affections consumed my every passion.

I divided my time into three distinct roles. Firstly, I was possibly the most important industrialist in the land. I again expanded my business horizons by investing heavily in the development of steam railways that Stella's father had forecast as the transportation of the future.

Starnes's interest had waned, but new inventive geniuses like Richard Trevithick and George Stephenson took his place. I was the largest shareholder in a new company, named the Stockton & Darlington Railway, now seeking a charter to haul goods or people by using men, horses or otherwise. The word "otherwise" meant by steam locomotion.

My life with Marjorie and the children developed into a pattern. Gone was the intimacy of sharing, for when home I was content to participate in those functions essential to our social standing.

Apart from that, Marjorie and the children seemed to occupy an island on which I was a stranger. There was some affection and respect, but an ever-widening gulf in interests made this less frequently displayed.

This gulf was diminished in importance by the presence of Stella. For the essence of Stella's being radiated an excitement and intimacy that precluded the need for the closeness of others.

We loved and laughed. We talked of business that Stella, unlike Marjorie, seemed to understand and take an interest in. I marveled at the clear, logical intelligence packed into her pretty head. Physically she was insatiable, draining my ardor so that the lack of any bodily relationship with Marjorie was a relief. Marjorie and I now occupied separate bedrooms by mutual consent. The pretext was we slept better. The real reason was our sexual incompatibility.

Months turned into years with amazing rapidity. I remembered my youth when the seasons seemed to last an eternity. I noticed the occasional gray hair mingling with the brown and lines forming around my eyes.

Marjorie was aging as well, but her beauty was being enhanced by the passage of time. In any gathering her regal bearing seemed dominant. She was greatly admired. Only a fool would fail to notice men gravitated to her like filings toward a magnet.

It never entered my mind that Marjorie and Stella might find other men interesting. Besides, I was much too engrossed in business to let such ludicrous thoughts disturb me.

It resembled a blow to the solar plexus when Mr. Hull, Stella's butler, confided she was having an affair.

He'd asked politely if he might speak to me in confidence. I had paid his bonus faithfully although, until now, there was nothing to report. He apologized profusely for having to give me such vexing news, but it was his duty.

My blood pressure rising, I pressed him for details. It was very furtive, Hull reported. Stella had recently been dismissing the servants early, saying that she was retiring for the night.

Mr. Hull, tired of reading but not sufficiently weary for bed, decided to walk in the garden one night when the moonlight flooded the landscape. He paused in the rose arbor as he heard footsteps stealthily approaching down the driveway.

A man emerged from the shadow of the trees and tiptoed toward the side entrance. Hull was about to voice a challenge when, to his amazement, the door opened and her ladyship, lamp in hand, ushered the man through the door.

Hull reentered the house to find it quiet. He'd expected, as her ladyship was entertaining, to be summoned to provide refreshments.

As there was no bell for his service, he tried sleeping, without success. As custodian of The Grange, it was his duty to ensure that her ladyship was safe. Wearily he dressed, then slipped upstairs to the section of the house where her ladyship slept.

Light under the door of Stella's room showed a candle burned in its mantle. But it was the sound inside the room that frightened him — a long moan as if someone was suffering.

Heart pounding, he debated whether to knock and demand if her ladyship was all right. The sounds and moaning intensified; so did the clearly audible creaking of the bed.

The sounds increased in speed and velocity as did gasps of fulfillment. In the silence that soon followed, Hull distinctly heard Stella say, "That was wonderful, darling."

Again Hull apologized for bringing me such sordid details. Curtly I requested he continue and questioned if this had been an isolated event?

Looking uncomfortable, he cleared his throat, "I wish I could tell you it was, your lordship, but I felt it my duty to determine if this were a continuing relationship.

"From that night on I watched from the window in the servants' hallway overlooking the side door. I'm unhappy to report, Sir, that the same man has returned frequently."

I thanked him for his information and asked him to pour me some scotch. "Shall I inform her ladyship of your presence?" he inquired. I replied this would not be necessary. I'd attend to that in my good time.

Stella was obviously sleeping, as I'd arrived much earlier than usual. I was glad of the fact. It provided time to collect my composure.

Hull's information exploded in my brain like a grenade, numbing my senses, creating rage. When first we undertook our arrangement, my mind occasionally dwelled on the young man Stella had mentioned.

As time passed, the memory faded. I felt as secure in my relationship with Stella as I did with Marjorie. Stella seemed more of a wife than Marjorie. I had thought we shared a relationship that would never be threatened, something so intimate, exciting and exhilarating that any possibility of it being breached was non-existent.

My screaming nerves thrust savage recollections into my red-misted memory: Stella's beauty, her passion, her intelligence, our first meeting, our joy of sharing, our common interests.

Then my imagination superimposed the vivid reality of another man thrusting in ecstasy into Stella's willing body, his enjoyment creating the moans of fulfillment I knew so well.

I downed the scotch and poured myself another. My first impulse had been to rush to Stella's room and confront her. As the alcohol burned its way down my throat, I realized I must compose myself.

Anger at my betrayal turned quickly to waves of hatred for the woman responsible. Stella, I vowed, would pay for her disloyalty.

I pulled the bell cord to summons Hull. This matter, I told him, must not be discussed. I would be leaving The Grange immediately, and under no circumstance should he inform her ladyship that I had been here.

Hull indicated he understood, again apologized for his role as the bearer of unpleasant news, and knowingly said he would again monitor events in my absence.

The lights of The Grange glowed yellow as I pointed my horse's head into the blackness of the night and the bleakness of despair.

I rode quickly through the wet mist, trying to place matters in perspective. At one point I rationalized that perhaps this situation was for the best. I was, after all, risking a great deal in pursuing my relationship with Stella.

Not that there was any chance of Marjorie discovering my infidelity, for I had covered my tracks very well. But still, there was a nominal hazard as there was in most ventures.

My mind created satisfying images of Stella in tears, pleading her case, swearing never again to compromise our relationship. Then my stern admonition it was too late. She would leave The Grange and my life forever.

Then another fantasy would crowd out the first: Stella and I again in ecstasy together as we had been so often. But the pleasure was always corrupted by the vivid picture of the other man, the creaking bed and her cries of delight.

CHAPTER 33

Disintegrating Dream

It was well past midnight as I slowed my horse to walk the half-mile circuit of the driveway leading to my home. I suspected Marjorie and the entire household had long since retired for the night. That was just as well; I was in no mood to talk.

Nobody would be expecting me at this hour. I made it a rule, whenever possible, to terminate my business trips with sufficient time to arrive home in the late afternoon or early evening.

With surprise I noted some windows bright with light.

I placed my tired horse in his loosebox before awakening a sleepy stable boy to attend to the animal. With minor apprehension, I entered the house by a side door.

Perhaps there was sickness in the house; that would be reason enough for lights. My fears were extinguished long before I reached the ballroom, for in the distance I could identify Marjorie's distinctive laughter. As the door to the ballroom was open, I paused in the comparative darkness of the hall to see who was being entertained. I was astounded to find only two people: Marjorie, with her back toward me and a man. It appeared to my disbelieving eyes that they were in the folds of an embrace.

I strode into the room. The man, ashen-faced, quickly pulled back. Marjorie turned her head to follow his stricken gaze, her hand rushing to her mouth, "Good God, George."

Muddied, tired and upset by the events of this horrendous day of cruel discovery, I was in no mood to be civil. "What in the name of God is going on here? Who in the hell is he?"

Marjorie turned as pale as a mist-enshrouded moon. "He . . . he . . ." she stammered, "is an old friend of my family, stationed in Canada with his regiment for the last five years. Being great friends when we were young, he decided to pay me. . . or us, I should say, a visit."

I hadn't noticed at first that he wore the uniform of a captain of the infantry of the 49th Regiment. I vaguely remembered Marjorie's father mentioning that some young acquaintance of his had fought with General Brock in repelling the American invasion of the colony in 1812.

The captain, now regaining some measure of his composure, clicked his heels together, came to attention and in a clear, strong voice announced, "Captain John Dennis, Sir, at your service."

I was in no mood for pleasantries. "You will do me a great service, Captain, if you will leave my house immediately," I snarled, "and as for you, Marjorie, I would like a thorough explanation."

The captain bowed stiffly and retreated through the door leading to the foyer. The massive door slammed and footsteps crunched along the pathway to the stable. Marjorie, in tears, rushed from the room.

My world, this morning so secure, was falling to pieces. Twice in less than six hours I had been brutalized by the disloyalty of those I loved most.

In Stella's case, there was no doubt of her infidelity. This in itself was enough to produce the acids of hatred churning through me. Now with Marjorie's apparent lack of propriety, if that is all it was, I was a man beset with fury at those who had deceived me.

Pouring myself a large drink, I proceeded to Marjorie's bedroom. I was determined before the night was over to find the truth. At first she refused me entry but, as my demands for an immediate audience grew louder, she called angrily to wait until she was ready.

I'd expected to find Marjorie in tears. Instead, she stood erect, her eyes defiant, her arms akimbo. My surprise allowed her to speak before I found words.

"I'm utterly ashamed of your disgraceful conduct," she spat, "but I suppose breeding will out." Never before had Marjorie spoken to me in this manner. I was aghast at the vehemence of her strident tone and cruel remark.

I was the one who should be on the attack, not she. The residual anger I suppressed for hours boiled over as I grasped her by the shoulders.

"You bloody bitch! You say you are ashamed of me. All I've done is return to my home, after days of hard work, to find you in the arms of some stupid soldier."

Events weren't happening the way I expected. Even in my anger, I thought she'd provide some believable explanation. The strain I was under proved too much. Rationality flew on the swift wings of seething rage. I shook her hard.

Although the force of my hands brought tears to her eyes, Marjorie smiled flint-hard. "Are you finished with your bullying bravado?" she asked, her voice sharp as a razor's edge.

"If so, I would ask you to remove your filthy hands from my shoulders. You are hurting me." Her demeanor quelled my fury momentarily and I released my grip.

Still intending to attack, I thought that I could obtain an advantage by proceeding in a more discreet manner. Without compassion, I said I was sorry for hurting her. She glowered, the dew of tears glistening on her cheeks, "You have been hurting me for ages. Why should you be sorry now?"

I protested the absurd accusation, pointing out with conviction this was the first time I'd laid a hand on her. I thought I had every right to do so. A sneering flicker of a smile creased her face.

"So you believe, George, this is the first time you've hurt me, do you? For your information, living with you has been hurtful for years."

I started to protest, but she continued, "You may be successful in business. You may be accepted socially, thanks in large part to my family and myself, but you are a complete failure as a husband and a father. All you give a damn about is making money and, of course, keeping that little tart of yours happy in that other house you occupy so frequently." It was as if I had fallen through ice into a freezing lake. My equilibrium seemed to fail, my legs became rubbery as the room slowly revolved. Marjorie's eyes, once so attractive, now glinted hard and hateful, piercing the armor of my alleged innocence, burning into the sanctum of my soul.

I protested my innocence; her accusations were ridiculous. They were a cover-up for the compromising situation in which I found her. If I were any judge of human nature, I shouted, she and her seedy captain friend had probably compromised to a far greater extent than in the ballroom.

Marjorie neither winced or protest her innocence. She stood regally erect, scarcely blinking, a frozen smile creasing her face.

"George, if your filthy imagination proves to be correct, what would you have me do with the long, lonely evenings I spend here while you are bedded down with your sweet Miss Starnes? Men do find me attractive, even if my charms play second fiddle to that little whore of yours."

Hopeless anger blended with fatigue and fear. The bedrock of wealth, success and prestige was crumbling into dust under my feet. My mind flickered as it groped for a solution. Should I plead for forgiveness?

I knew the power of Marjorie's family. If my indiscretions became common knowledge, I would be ruined socially. And what good was wealth if you were shunned in the halls of power? My inclination was to smash her imperious face, but I hesitated in fear of reprisal.

Crushing despair forced the fight from me. I had to preserve the most important thing in my life, the Humphrey enterprises. Nothing else mattered. "What am I then to do, Marjorie?" I asked. "Is there anything that can be done?"

I stood naked, eyes downcast, stripped of my manhood. "Things will never be as they once were with you and me, George," replied Marjorie. "You have destroyed all the loving feelings I once felt for you. You have traded me and the children for your lust for wealth and acclaim.

"Our relationship cooled and you didn't notice. All that remained was the outer shell of pretense with a rotting core. All you can do now is rid us of that concubine of yours so her shadow will never cast its darkness into our lives again."

Hope created a small hole in the clouds of agony. "Do you mean things will be as they once were? These events will be forgotten?"

"Never will these deplorable actions of yours be forgotten by me," she said. "And never will our relationship be the same. Still, if you do as I say, the charade we have been living as man and wife will continue. More important to you, your standing in the community and amongst your peers will be maintained."

Although tired beyond description, humiliated, furious and frightened, it was not until dawn, aided by a bottle of whisky, that I would sleep, an un-refreshing, nightmare-punctuated sleep.

Staggering from dampened sheets to the window, I judged it was well past noon. The events of yesterday filled me with anger, then flooded my befuddled brain with reality. There was no escape from the route I must take. There was only one thing of supreme importance that must be preserved at all costs: the Humphrey enterprises.

I was no longer in love with Marjorie, I admitted. She was beautiful, witty and popular. She'd been my key in unlocking the gate of the social acceptance, and played a continuing role in the important relationships necessary to maintain.

Finding her in the arms of another man was not so much a blow to my emotions as it was to my pride. I realized in the grayness of the afternoon her indiscretions were of little consequence since they never interfered with my success. Satisfying Marjorie's demands would be easy.

Stella.... I vowed to return her to the mediocrity from where she came. The passion and sense of belonging she'd engendered quickly turned to bitter hatred. I looked forward to implementing my revenge.

That evening I found it easy to accept the curtain of cold detachment Marjorie assumed. She been quite correct in demanding I divest myself of Stella, I admitted. I'd been extremely foolish.

For the well being of ourselves and our children we must preserve our social standing, as it reflected on the business. The terms of our relationship, as she had spelled them out, I agreed were acceptable to me.

The following day I promised to implement the salient point: getting rid of Stella. There was no smile, no warmth, not the slightest spark of enthusiasm as Marjorie listened. "That is exactly what I thought you would say," she said without apparent interest.

CHAPTER 34

Fear and Fury

As my carriage sped toward The Grange, I felt a perverse sense of satisfaction in knowing Stella was about to pay dearly for her actions. For she'd changed. No longer was she the eager "do gooder" of past years.

She was now a woman of great leisure, enjoying to the utmost the wealth I provided. She'd become rather lazy, depending almost entirely upon her servants for everything. Of course, this is what I had intended and persistently encouraged.

My strategy had been to change her from the dedicated charity worker, always worrying about others, to the woman she'd become . . . vulnerable and dependent entirely upon me.

My plan backfired like a rusty cannon. Her leisure gave her the inclination to indulge in a pleasure I'd never expected: another man.

I could see Stella, her eyes full of tears, imploring me to recant my decision to vanquish her from my life and The Grange. The mental picture filled me with satisfaction. As I'd suffered through humiliation, those responsible for my agony would suffer more.

I ordered the driver to stop so I could provide myself with a substantial amount of money. My intent was to pay the servants before dismissing them from service.

The idea rankled, but Stella, too, would have to be provided with money to reestablish herself. She could no longer return home to her father due to his recent death.

Bestowing money on Stella was comparable to rewarding a thief who'd stolen from me. Still, it was necessary as I wished to prevent gossip that George Humphrey was responsible for making a woman destitute. The amount would be sufficient to provide food and lodging for two to three months.

Being Friday, Stella would not be expecting me. My visits inevitably took place in the middle of the week. Saturdays were reserved for completing work at my office; Sunday was always for my obligatory appearance at Saint John's Church with my family.

My visit I wanted to be a complete surprise to Stella. I would appear unannounced, pretend that our relationship remained as it was. She would, I imagined, ask why I hadn't made my usual midweek visit . . . the night Hull informed me of her unfaithfulness.

For the last time, I wanted to feel her thrusting body, see those beautiful, passionate eyes peering into my mine. Then, I would hurl her from me and expose my knowledge of her deceit. After her shocked horror, I envisaged, would come the pleading and tears. Perhaps even a denial. I would crush it with the irrefutable facts that Hull had provided.

As we approached the vicinity of The Grange, I ordered the driver to stop the carriage at a small inn less than a mile from country house. He was to wait for me, as my business might take sometime. My reason for proceeding on foot was to avoid the clattering wheels announcing my arrival.

I let myself in by the front door and with a pounding heart, swiftly climbed the stairs toward her bedchamber. No servants were in evidence as I quickly moved down the broad hall.

I knocked our secret code, three sharp raps repeated twice. Stella would know immediately it was me, not her maid.

"George, darling, is that you?" Stella gasped. I confirmed it was to a profound silence. After perhaps a minute, Stella asked me to wait until she'd made herself presentable. "I didn't expect you, darling. I never really bother about my appearance when you're not here."

I heard her rush about the room, surmising she was dressing or combing her hair. I waited patiently, savoring the effect it would have being told her days of leisure were over, that this evening she would vacate The Grange and my life forever.

"George," she opened the door and rushed into my arms, "I've missed you so much. Why didn't you arrive Tuesday or Wednesday as you usually do?"

For a brief moment, her ardor appeared so genuine I nearly reciprocated by kissing her and pulling her clinging body tighter to mine. Then, with the vomit of bitterness clogging my throat, I shoved her back into the room, slamming the door behind us. The composure I'd hoped to maintain burst like a soap bubble. The passions of fury and betrayal I'd tried to suppress so agonizingly burst with the force of gun powder. "You cheating whore! You ungrateful wench!"

I pushed her roughly toward the bed, ripping her dress. "You thought you could deceive me, didn't you? You thought I would provide The Grange and this life-style so you could have numerous lovers."

I thrust her on the bed, her terrified eyes staring at me as if I'd gone mad. Straddling her body, my hands tightened on her neck. "You rotten bitch! You've ruined my life."

The frustration of events so rapidly befalling me culminated in a sea of loathing for the woman who lay beneath me. She tried to speak but the pressure of my hands on her throat permitted only a rasping gurgle. Freeing one hand, I slapped at her crimson face with unrepentant fury.

Return Passage

My groin erupted in flaming agony as Stella thrust her knee upward, catching me hard in the testicles. Momentarily imprisoned in a straitjacket of inertia, I crouched by the bed in a vortex of blinding pain.

I was vaguely aware of Stella attempting to escape to the door. As the fog of pain began to recede, I realized somebody was swiftly approaching from the rear. Turning my head, I saw a pair of riding boots. Above them, arose a giant of a man with the malevolent appearance of death in his dark eyes.

Some primitive sense of self-preservation sent a signal obliterating pain and confusion. I rose to my feet and lithely stepped to one side as the giant rushed toward me.

I was no match for this man who outweighed and towered above me. Instinctively, I grasped the nearest object, a heavy brass candle stick.

Undeterred, the giant rushed toward me. Crouching, I swung my weapon, smashing him across his throat. He dropped like a pheasant, producing rasping sounds as he fought for breath.

I'd forgotten Stella, who, with a piercing shriek of anguish, began clawing my face with razor-sharp nails. Again I swung the candle stick. Stella fell across the bed, blood oozing from her mangled face. Her beauty fled; she lay still, her eyes lifeless and dull, her breasts bare and without form.

Stillness descended upon the room. The giant ceased his gasping, his glazed eyes staring at a corner of the bedroom, away from Stella. Stella stared directly upward, her dark eyes becoming bluish. Both were dead.

I giggled, roared with laughter, then cried. I longed for the womb, the security of the unborn, the innocence of birth. The world closed upon me, crushing me in its conventional law and retribution.

Resentment against the fools who dictated right from wrong filled me. Panic and fear, resentment and resolution, abhorrence and acceptance of my situation flashed through my mind in disjointed sequences. I stood, lonely in space and time. I was a fox surrounded by a pack of hounds.

My thinking process cleared. Had the servants seen me enter The Grange or been alerted by the noise? It was highly unlikely.The servants occupied rooms to the side and rear of the building. It was only a fortuitous circumstance that initially led Hull to encounter Stella's lover on his evening walk.

If Hull or any other servants had been aware of the commotion, surely they would have rushed to the room. At any rate, that would have to be determined later.

My mind raced; I must hide my crime. The only solution was to make it appear that Stella and her lover had had a violent quarrel, resulting in their deaths.

Picking up the blood-smeared candlestick, I placed it in the broad hand of the huge man, as if he'd wielded the weapon. While I was doing this, I noticed he was unmarked except for the bruise on his throat. The authorities would question how Stella had killed him.

I cast my eyes over the room in desperation; there had to be a logical way of explaining his death. Then I saw it lying on the writing table, a long letter opener. Twice I plunged it deep into the man's chest before curling Stella's lifeless fingers around the handle.

It looked convincing. Obviously a violent and tragic lover's quarrel that had ended in tragedy. Thoroughly I checked the scene. There was nothing to connect me with events.

I realized the police investigation would involve me and that would be unpleasant. However, as far as I could see, there was not a shred of evidence that I had been in The Grange this evening, other than a chance sighting by the servants.

Stealthily as a stalking cat, I peered into the quiet hallway before furtively proceeding down the stairway and out of the house. All was still. Quickly I crossed into the trees bordering the driveway, keeping in their shadows until the road jogged out of sight.

I walked swiftly back the way I'd come. Barely an hour had passed. Within twelve minutes I was back at the inn.

I glanced into the public bar and, to my relief, saw my driver with a pint of beer in front of him, deep in conversation with another man. I crossed the lobby to ask the manager of the inn if I could rent facilities to wash.

"I had a losing argument with some brambles. Lost my way taking a shortcut through the woods." The man, who at first had looked critically at my bloodied face, now broke into a friendly smile as I pushed a sovereign toward his outstretched hand.

"Very good, Sir," he said respectfully. "If you'll follow me, I'll soon have a towel and a jug of hot water brought to this room." I washed and examined my face. With the crusted blood removed, only small superficial abrasions remained that, as I just claimed, could have been inflicted by sharp brambles. Unless one examined my face by a closely held lamp, as I had done, it was probable that the small cuts would go unnoticed.

Leaving the inn by the main entrance, I intended to stride boldly into the public bar through the street door and summon my driver. As it was, we almost collided as I was turning the corner of the inn.

"I was just seeing to the horse, your Lordship," he said. "Have you completed your business, Sir?" I informed him most of it was complete. There was one last errand left. I gave him directions to The Grange before we clattered into the night.

CHAPTER 35

Checkmate

Loud knocking on the main door eventually produced the sight of lamps being lit within the darkened house. The footman's voice demanded who was calling. I answered that it was me. I'd lost my keys.

He apologized for his tardiness, stating Mr. Hull had taken the evening off as he had doubted there would be work to do tonight. A wave of relief swept through me. Hull, at least, would not have seen me and by the demeanor of the footman, I doubted if anybody else had either.

"Then all has been quiet?" I asked. "What about your mistress?" She had dismissed her maid soon after supper, he replied politely, adding Stella said she was suffering from a headache and wouldn't require anything tonight.

It would be better if somebody other than I discovered the bodies, I thought. "Will you get the maid," I ordered. "Perhaps Miss Starnes will require the help of a female if she's ill."

The maid approached, smoothing her uniform. "I think it prudent you ask Miss Starnes if she is well enough to see me," I said with concern. "Meanwhile," I said to the footman who'd returned, "will you be good enough to bring me a scotch and water?"

I'd had time for a sip before a chilling scream echoed through the house. I rushed up the broad staircase, followed by the footman, toward the sounds of fear. The maid stood transfixed, her hands clutching her head, her frenzied eyes bulging from her head.

It was crucial I play my part well, I realized.

"Quickly," I snapped to the footman, "get water and towels! There's been some dreadful accident! You," I bellowed at the maid, "stop sniveling and check your mistress."

I bent over the prostrate giant, placing my hand over his heart. "My God, I believe he's dead!" I shouted, before rising quickly to rush to where Stella lay. Pushing the maid aside, I acted out my charade, checking for a heartbeat.

Waiting long enough for the breathless footman to enter the room with the water and towels, I went into my next act. "Lord!" I whispered hoarsely, "what's that in Miss Starnes' hand?"

Both servants stared in horror at the letter opener.

No act was necessary to enhance emotion, for I was shaken by the carnage I'd caused in Stella's chambers. The servants were devastated. Looking sternly at the cowering footman, I demanded to know whether he had heard anything because there surely must have been a terrible racket.

He quickly assured me that he hadn't heard a thing, adding that the servant's quarters are far removed from this wing of the house. A sense of relief swept through me. I definitely hadn't been seen or heard.

I continued my questioning. Had either servant remembered seeing this dead man? No, they replied. I then surmised the man had been a thief, for their benefit. "I believe we should get the authorities. Will you have the groom saddle a horse and ride at once to the nearest police station?"

Meanwhile, I instructed, the door was to be locked and nobody should be allowed in. I added that this situation was so distressing to me I would go at once to the nearby inn, where the authorities could find me, if necessary.

Another fearful night I spent in anguish. The ghosts of Stella and her dead lover seemed to sigh through my darkened room. Sudden flashes of Stella's lifeless face and staring eyes punctuated the black night.

The quarterly-hour chime of some distant clock marked the dismal passage of time. The bottle of scotch I had taken from The Grange was empty, and still sleep eluded me.

More terrifying were the visions of myself on trial, found guilty, incarcerated and hanged, though I reminded myself, forcefully, that these apocalyptic nightmares were an impossibility.

Everything last night had gone smoothly. There wasn't a shred of evidence to convict me. The servants, I was positive, would vouch that my relationship with Stella was warm and loving.

The summons I expected didn't arrive until after lunch. A police constable called to say that Colonel Hathaway of the County Police awaited my pleasure at The Grange.

Rounding up my coachman, who again was in the bar, I made the short jaunt to the house. A robust man who introduced himself as Colonel Hathaway, Chief Constable of the Durham County Constabulary, greeted me.

The Colonel came directly to the point. "I'm sure this tragic event has been a great blow to you, your Lordship, and I'm sorry to have to bother you. You must be upset. It's a grisly business we are investigating and, I'm sure, you wish to get to the bottom of it, as we do."

Colonel Hathaway, although in civilian clothes, had the unmistakable look of the professional soldier. He had probably earned his constabulary rank by distinguished service in the army.

His eyes, intelligent, dominating, peered from a handsome face enhanced by an aquiline nose and a waxed mustache. He cleared his throat, looking embarrassed. "It appears, Sir, that due to this unfortunate event, I must ask you some personal questions."

He'd done his homework. It was quickly evident he knew of my relationship with Stella. I readily admitted that what he concluded was correct. The Colonel, in an understanding, gentlemanly way, expressed the hope that his investigations wouldn't impinge upon my relationship with my wife and family.

"It shouldn't," he said, smiling grimly. "This grisly mess seems to exclude you completely, other than the deep sense of loss you must feel concerning the death of Miss Starnes."

A wave of relief gently parted the fog of fear within me. Colonel Hathaway continued, "You will understand that I must ask you some questions about your whereabouts last night at the time of the murders."

Agreeing this was a necessity, I asked him how he'd determined when the killings took place. He smiled thinly before replying.

"I really had nothing to do with estimating the time of death. We are very fortunate in Durham county to have a very good doctor, vitally interested in any sort of homicide. He has been of great assistance to us in the past in determining the time of and cause of deaths.

"He was here this morning and took both bodies for examination in his surgery before turning them over to the undertaker. He estimates the deaths took place early yesterday evening."

"The footman," he glanced at a small notebook, "Mr. Doubleday, informs us, your Lordship, that you arrived at this house at approximately nine o'clock. Is that correct?" I nodded assent.

"He tells us that you sent for the maid and ordered her to Miss Starnes' quarters since you were concerned about her welfare as she had complained about a headache earlier?" I nodded.

The Colonel looked at his notes before continuing. "Then you and the footman, Doubleday, heard the maid scream, rushed to her aid and discovered the bodies. Is that correct, Sir?" I assured him that it was.

The Colonel stared into space, seemingly oblivious to me or the ticking of the large clock. Finally breaking his silence, he asked me quietly if Miss Starnes and myself were on the best of terms. A dagger of alarm pierced my gut.

Feigning surprise, I answered that, of course, our relationship was warm and extremely close. "Do you believe, for one moment, Colonel, that I would risk so much if this were not so?"

He studied my face intently before continuing. "There are a few minor details that puzzle the good doctor and myself. The first thing is that the dead man, although stabbed twice in the chest, didn't bleed from the wound, which seems very strange.

"The other thing is that Miss Starnes had minute shreds of skin under her finger nails. She must have scratched somebody violently, and yet, there wasn't the slightest scratch on the dead man's person."

A cold fear clutched at my innards, momentarily turning me into a helpless rag doll. The Colonel's eyes glinted triumphantly under their shaggy brows.

"Where did you get those tiny blemishes on your face, your Lordship? Those marks could have easily resulted from a woman's finger nails." I jumped to my feet, crashing the chair to the floor. Fear of discovery fueled the anger pouring from my mouth. "Just who in hell do you think you are talking to?" I demanded.

"Could you possibly believe that a Lord of the Realm, perhaps the most important man in northern England, would go around murdering people, and to what purpose? I will see that you rue the day for such an asinine accusation."

Colonel Hathaway rose to his feet to stand facing me. "I am accusing you of nothing, Sir," he retorted rapier-like. "I am merely carrying out my duty. Now, if you will be good enough to sit, I would like my question answered. Those marks on your face, how did you get them?"

My mind functioned as if enmeshed in thick tar. No logical explanation emerged. I groped bleakly to think of a plausible answer, then returned helplessly into the initial account I'd given the innkeeper. I'd fallen into brambles.

The Colonel seemed to accept this without argument. Then his rapier prodded another soft spot. "When did this happen?" he demanded.

Like a fly ensnared in some horrible web, I told him that it was early last evening. He could, I said, check with the man at the inn. He would verify I'd asked him for hot water and a place to clean myself.

He nodded his head, again studying his notebook. "Yes, you are correct about that. Mr. Ramsbottom, the inn keeper, remembers you clearly. Also the sovereign you gave him for so modest a service.

"He informs me that to the best of his recollection this request of yours for hot water and a place to wash took place at eight o'clock. Would you say that this is correct, your Lordship?"

Agreeing this was possible, I stated I hadn't noticed the time. Again Colonel Hathaway consulted his pocket-sized leather notebook. Clearing his throat, his pointed finger traced words penned within. "Your driver tells us you arrived at the inn late in the afternoon, about an hour before sundown. That would be about five o'clock at this time of year. Is that correct, Sir?"

Perspiration flowed down my body. Slowly, methodically, this monster of a man was backing me into a corner from which there appeared to be no escape. I acknowledged his question by a slight nod.

"If, as you have suggested, you arrived in the district at approximately five o'clock, may I ask you what business you did from the time you arrived at five until the time you ordered your driver to transport you to The Grange?"

My mind refused to function with the speed and precision I expected. Desperately, I groped for some logical explanation of the more than three hours supposedly spent on business.

I was positive my driver had informed the Colonel how he'd waited in the public bar for my return. I lacked any choice other than sticking to my story.

I cleared my constricting throat while trying to appear calm. "In fact, Colonel, the business engaged in is of a confidential nature. I trust the details I'm about to divulge will go no further?

"You realize I have business interests all over northern England. My reputation and wealth is common knowledge. If I try to buy land from someone, they assume I can afford to pay any amount. Often, this inflates the asking price.

"I've been toying with the idea of building a new factory on land near the inn. I had only glanced at it superficially, either mounted on horseback or from the window of a carriage. Last evening I took the opportunity of minutely examining the land on foot to see if it met with my specifications. Unfortunately, darkness closed in before I had completed my task."

Colonel Hathaway's eyes bored into mine without as much as a flicker of his eyelids. "So if I understand you, Sir," he said, "you were reconnoitering the land to consider buying it, if it seemed suitable for your purposes. Is that correct?" I assured him that it was.

"Around six the sun set and it grew dark. Still, it wasn't until just before nine that you met your driver and ordered him to take you to The Grange, is that also correct?" I agreed it was. Colonel Hathaway's voice became a low monotone. "Could you explain to me what you were doing for two hours in the darkness?"

I forced a strained laugh. "You may have difficulty believing this, Colonel Hathaway, but I became absolutely lost in that dense wood bordering the road."

The Colonel didn't seem amused. "Do you mean to tell me that you were lost in a wood covering no more than twenty acres for over two hours?" he asked with the slightest nuance of sarcasm. "Yes," I admitted. "I feel like a complete idiot, but it is the truth. You can ask the inn keeper. I told him about it when I explained I had fallen into the brambles."

Colonel Hathaway snorted in reply while again consulting his notebook. His next question veered completely off course and was not at all what I had envisaged. "Why do you think a man could be stabbed in the chest and not bleed?"

I thought hard before answering. "Perhaps because the heart was destroyed so that there would be no blood pressure?" "That is a possibility," replied the Colonel, "or could it be that the man was dead already and the murderer merely stabbed a corpse?"

My legs felt like slack rope as Colonel Hathaway's eyes burned into mine. "You see, Sir, the doctor reports that the man's trachea was crushed. That would cause death by strangulation, like hanging from a gallows."

It was like being devoured by quicksand. Slowly, cruelly, my defenses were overwhelmed by these sinister questions provided by Colonel Hathaway's notebook. It was almost as if I floated above my body watching some grotesque play in which I performed a leading part.

As if mesmerized, I heard the Colonel's next question wafting in my direction with the softness of thistledown, yet containing within its gentleness the sting of death. "You, of course, know Miss Starnes' butler, Mr. Hull. Did you realize while you say you were lost in the woods, he and your driver drank together in the public bar of the inn?"

My God! I realized, with horror, my driver had been sitting with a man whose back was toward me. I thought he looked vaguely familiar, although at the time other more important things filled my mind. It had been Hull.

"And do you know that Mr. Hull informed your driver that you had gone to The Grange? He saw you enter by the front door just as he turned the corner of the house on his way to the inn."

I bolted for the door, knocking the Colonel and his chair backward as I did so. As surely as a rabbit in a trap, I was caught. I was running for my life. Nothing else now mattered. Nothing I could say could prevent the truth from surfacing.

Hull would surely tell all when questioned: my knowledge of Stella's lover, my orders to him to say nothing. Nothing could help me. Not my wealth, my power, my children, nor Marjorie. For in our sterile relationship, she was as dead as Stella.

I heard Colonel Hathaway bellowing that I was to be stopped, but he was too late. My carriage and horses still stood where we'd recently left them. Leaping upon the driver's seat, I released the brake, flicked the long whip across the backs of the horses, sending them careening down the circular driveway into the fading sunlight.

My mind, recently so fuzzy, now regenerated its ability for clear, precise thought. Immediately a plan began taking shape. I still had the bulk of the money I'd brought with me yesterday. It was enough, at least, to buy passage on a ship bound for some far off land.

I didn't care what direction it took me — Australia, North America, anywhere where English is spoken. I realized swift pursuit was inevitable. I must change identity, my clothing and my mode of transportation.

At the inn I had recently left, I reigned in my heavily-breathing horses and leapt to the ground. A good-looking horse was tethered to a hitching post, still saddled and bridled. In less than a minute I had tightened the girths, mounted and galloped full tilt down the road.

Liverpool, I decided, would be my destination. I should, with luck, arrive sometime tomorrow. Meanwhile, I must cover my tracks by changing horses, travelling by coach and even using the newly built Manchester to Liverpool railway.

I rode all night and well into the dawn before stopping for breakfast. From the keeper of the roadhouse I purchased rough clothing for my transformation from a gentleman to a working man, one of the thousands who inhabited this part of England.

Donning worker's clothing disguised the look of prosperity. Again I was Tom Brown, although this time there would be no respite from the role I must play.

CHAPTER 36

New World — Fresh Start

Arriving in Liverpool, I mingled undetected with the hundreds of other working people. My early days of training were paying dividends. Emerging as Tom Brown, even with the intervening years of power and prosperity, was like donning old, familiar clothing. Mirthlessly, I considered what my father's reaction would have been if he knew of my deeds and deception. I felt increasingly confident. There was little chance of apprehension while in Liverpool.

Colonel Hathaway would give chase with the discovery of the missing horse from the inn. The trail would grow cold as he and his men lacked any idea of the direction I was travelling.

Eventually, the horse I'd stolen would be found. Its location would show I was heading westward. Fortunately, the mails were slow and I was sure I could find passage long before a search was initiated.

Three ships were due to sail within the next few hours, one eastward bound, the other two westward. I preferred the latter direction. I took a room in a small hotel frequented by those who sailed in steerage.

I found the opportunity I sought. Two men talked with animation of the new life awaiting them in Canada. When they parted company, I approached the younger, saying I had a proposition to discuss I was sure would be of great interest.

Apprehensive at first, he eventually agreed to accompany me to a nearby pub, as I said it could mean substantial money. My tale of torment flowed as easily as if it were true.

I'd inherited a modest amount of money from my uncle's estate. My wife, the bane of my life, a shrilling shrew, dominated my existence, casting her ugly shadow between me and the happiness I sought.

My only child, a daughter, had emigrated to Canada with her husband. Her main reason for doing so was to escape the clutches of her dominating mother. The secondary one was to seek opportunity in a new land.

My inheritance could be my passport to freedom, if only I could arrange immediate passage to Canada. If this took too long, my wife would figure out my plan by having the shipping records checked. She would set legal machinery in motion to have me deported from Canada to stand trial for desertion. I'd discovered the young man was travelling alone without family ties or encumbrances. If only he would permit me to change places with him, I would not only reimburse the money paid for his passage, I'd double the amount.

All he must do is provide me with his ticket and passport to assume his identity. He could, I assured him, book passage again within a week, and arrive in Canada with a sizeable amount of money.

Warily the young man eyed me. I felt he believed my story until I suggested I take his place aboard ship using his name. He became alarmed.

Hastily, I pulled the bag of sovereigns from my inner pocket, poured them into my hand so his eyes could feast upon them. As I had expected, his wariness changed to longing.

Quickly I pressed my advantage. He could easily explain to the ship's owners about a robbery of his papers and passage. There would be no trouble. He could book a new passage immediately, arriving in Canada a week or two later than planned, with a substantial amount of money to establish himself.

He had nothing to lose and everything to gain. I felt sure his decision would be in my favor, but just to be positive I added the clincher. "I'll give you more money, on one condition: if you promise never to divulge our arrangement, no matter what the circumstances.

"If I have your word you'll never describe or involve me, I'll give you three times the amount of your passage, plus providing sufficient money to live until you sail." He stuck his hand out to be shaken; the deal was made.

Early next morning, as John Cummins, with papers and passage carefully scrutinized, I boarded ship. The purser assigned my berth on the West Star for the long, rough and uncomfortable journey to Canada.

The vessel began to roll when we cleared harbor. More than a hundred and fifty of us crowded into the hull with neither portholes nor windows providing light.

Rows of berths lined both sides of the bulkhead. Long tables and benches down the center were the furnishings. The only illumination came from two lamps. The meals, consisting of salt pork and bread, barely edible the first few days of the voyage, soon turned rancid and sour.

We received one quart of water a day for drinking. There was no provision for washing. The days and weeks dragged by in misery. The voyage was often extremely rough and I was not a good sailor.

Much of this time I lay on my bunk too sick to move. Still, there were problems far more serious. Some passengers were dying of cholera, if the ship's doctor diagnosed it correctly. The bodies were quickly removed for a brief service and burial at sea. It would be cruel fate if I were to contract the plague after all my efforts and adventures.

More than twenty of my fellow passengers and one or two sailors had died already. I managed to survive. A feeling of hope and welcome relief flooded over me when we saw the wooded hills of the Gaspe from the Gulf of the St. Lawrence.

The miserable six-week journey was ending. A new life, in a new world, with new challenges was about to begin.

My knowledge of Canada was superficial. I didn't know how I would provide for myself. If desperate, I could always fall back on the broad knowledge gained in my early days as a working man.

It was a pleasant surprise to find that a person with administrative talents and a knowledge of business could rapidly succeed in this new and vibrant land. Once landed on Canadian soil, the John Cummins of the steerage class became John Cummins, an educated gentleman. It would be a simple thing to fabricate a convincing story concerning my past to suit my requirements.

Travelling to Upper Canada, I established myself in York, soon renamed Toronto. At first I was content to work at anything available. Soon, I discovered, there were many ways of earning a good living if one could establish oneself with the right people.

Already there was political trouble in the colony. A crusading publisher by the name of William Lyon Mackenzie was promoting government reform in his paper, *The Colonial Advocate.*

Claiming the Lieutenant Governor was manipulated by a powerful group of the establishment, lining their pockets at the expense of the new settlers, he demanded change.

His charges were probably correct, but I had learned success lay not with championing the cause of the underdogs, but with those who wielded power.

Skillfully, I fostered the acquaintance of these powerbrokers, called "The Family Compact." It was time, I suggested, that Mackenzie be put in his place and the way to do that was to smash his office and presses.

Many agreed in principle but were loathe to associate themselves with such a venture. I assured them their participation would not be required. They could distance themselves from such an undertaking if they would leave things to me.

All it took was a few visits to local drinking establishments and the price of many whiskeys to recruit sufficient young thugs for the job. Although the smashing of MacKenzie's presses was only a temporary setback for him and his reformers, it established me as a friend to the rich and powerful.

With their assistance and my business skills, John Cummins became recognized as one who had come to the colony and succeeded in climbing the ladder of success.

The horrors faded from my mind. Rarely, these days, did my thoughts retrace the events leading up to my escape from England. Nor did the loss of prestige and power still rankle. I was forging a new life that, in some ways, surpassed the old. In Upper Canada I was building a new business empire entirely on my merits.

With financial backing from my friends, I used my considerable business acumen to satisfy the needs of an expanding community. I pioneered new fields of endeavor in the real estate market and established several retail stores.

I provided myself with a handsome new home on Yonge Street, second only in size and prestige to those owned by the old establishment. With my rapid success in the world of business came complete acceptance by the leading lights of society.

I didn't need a Marjorie to foster my respectability here. Toronto, as it had become, was a thriving, exciting and expanding community with a vigorous social life. I met Mary Sinclair, recently widowed and wealthy.

Mary reminded me of Stella's dark-eyed beauty, and Marjorie's regal bearing and impeccable manners. It was my hope that before long we would marry as there was no barrier to such a union.

As John Cummins, I was free as a cloud, without encumbrances. Mary, once she had waited for a period of time considered proper after her husband's death, was as keen as I to tie the nuptial knot.

When I'd first arrived in Canada, I purchased many English newspapers to see if there were any mention of the events from which I'd escaped. I found many stories at first.

"Lord of the Realm, prime suspect in grisliest murder, a leader of industry," they wrote. This type of scandal was of great interest to those whose business is misfortune. There were a couple of interviews with Colonel Hathaway, who, it seems, suspected that I had set sail for foreign shores.

There was even the suggestion that I had perhaps used the name Tom Brown in my escape. Gradually, mention of me became less frequent, and relegated to the back pages.

As the stories diminished in size and importance, so did fears of capture. Four thousand miles of land and sea were an effective safeguard, I reasoned. I now even looked different, having nurtured a full beard. I doubted there was need to worry.

CHAPTER 37

Fickle Fate

The Lieutenant Governor's Ball was the social event of the year, so I became delighted when an imposing, engraved invitation arrived. More pleasing, I learned Mary would attend. Somebody on the Lieutenant Governor's staff was knowledgeable about the social happenings of the community. Obviously, Mary and I should share each other's company. A joint invitation would have been out of the question.

Feelings of pride and satisfaction intermingled as my carriage joined the slow procession of vehicles dispatching occupants at the door of the brilliantly lighted Vice Regal mansion. Scarlet-clad doormen helped guests from their carriages. Somewhere in the garden a band played martial music.

Slowly, we filed through the opened doors to present our invitations to an impressive major-domo. In thundering voice, he announced our names so we could proceed to pay our respects to the Lieutenant Governor, his wife and members of his staff.

That completed, I proceeded down the line, nodding to dignitaries comprising the official welcoming party. The next to last person was a tall man in uniform with the rank of lieutenant colonel.

It was like being struck by a bolt of lightening. There stood John Dennis, the onetime captain whom I had caught in embrace with Marjorie in the ballroom. Fear rose like acid in my throat while perspiration gushed from every pore. Only with supreme effort could I control my instinct to dash from the room. I could do nothing but continue to the area where the laughing, carefree guests assembled.

Had Dennis recognized me? I doubted it, seeing no flicker of recognition in his eyes. I glanced back fearfully, half expecting him to be looking my way. He wasn't, his attention riveted exclusively on a young, beautifully-gowned woman with blonde hair.

As the ball progressed my fears subsided. Colonel Dennis vanished, swallowed by the crowd. Meeting Mary, I began to relax, enjoying the lively music and dancing. The excellent food, generous liquor supply, and Mary sparkling in gaiety dispelled the uneasiness completely.

My feeling of security was so overwhelming before the night ended, I made a point of engaging Colonel Dennis in brief conversation. I asked about his military career and his present posting. He was both polite and charming.

Slightly intoxicated but implicitly happy with the events of the evening, I arrived home, had a large nightcap and prepared for bed. Tomorrow, I had arranged to meet Mary to spend a leisurely afternoon picnicking by the lake.

Just as I entered the wonderful, drifting world of fleeting presleep imagery, I returned to groggy wakefulness by a loud banging on the front door.

I lay hoping a servant would be awakened by the noise and attend to whoever was calling. When it was apparent all slept as if entombed, I crawled from the warmth of my bed. Pulling my dressing gown tightly against the late night chill, I descended the stairs.

Sliding the heavy night bolt back, I opened the door the few inches the safety chain permitted. In the darkness there appeared to be three men, none of whom I recognized. Irritably, I asked what they wanted.

The larger of the three demanded authoritatively to know if I were Mr. John Cummins. I acknowledged I was. "And are you the Mr. Cummins who accompanied Mrs. Mary Sinclair to the Lieutenant Governor's Ball this evening?"

Again, I said I was, although I corrected him by stating that although in Mrs. Sinclair's company almost exclusively, I had not accompanied her to the event.

The man heard me out in silence, then in a somber voice as dark as the night, informed me that unfortunately he was the bearer of bad news.

My pulse raced. All I could think of was Mary. Had she had an accident? Why else would these men come banging on my door? I fumbled with the safety chain, inviting them to enter.

Two burly men in police uniforms pushed by me; the third seemed to have vanished. I waved them into the parlor, lit the lamp on a table and faced the smaller man, who'd done all the talking. "Well, what is your news?" I asked fearfully.

"Please sit, Sir. This will take a little time to explain." I did as he suggested, impatient for his message. He stood facing me grimly, his companion placing a hand upon my shoulder in what I assumed was a gesture of sympathy.

Clearing his throat, the policeman began to speak. "It seems there has been a dreadful accident in which two people lost their lives. One was a young man, the other an attractive woman."

A picture of an overturned carriage leapt into my mind, Mary lying crushed. "However," he continued, "it was not an accident at all but premeditated murder, wouldn't you say, your Lordship?"

My mind whirled in a grotesque state of shock. How had this happened? Who could possibly wish to kill Mary and some man? I began stammering the questions pouring into my mind....

With the suddenness of a clap of thunder in a cloudless sky, it struck home. The policeman had not said "Sir" or "Mr. Cummins". He had used the title so familiar in my past, "Your Lordship."

Terrified, I futilely attempted to leap to my feet against the powerful grip of the larger policeman. Immobilized, I realized the game had ended. I made no protest as the steel handcuffs closed over my wrists.

The living nightmare would last for over six months. My confession read that I was George Humphrey, created Lord Durham by the pleasure of his late Majesty. What else could I say?

I learned that Lieutenant Colonel John Dennis had recognized me and had been aware of my escape from England. He had been asked by Colonel Hathaway to keep his eyes open for me in the colonies, in the faint chance I'd travelled to Canada.

His military discipline enabled him to maintain composure when he spoke to me. Dennis, I learned, had informed the police of his suspicions before the Ball had ended. The officer in charge devised the plan of waiting to apprehend me in the middle of the night, believing I'd be least alert and more easily confused at that time. The third policeman, the one who had seemed to vanish, was sent to the rear entrance in case I tried to escape.

The policemen placed me in the Black Maria, which clattered roughly toward the fortress prison beside the Don River. Leg irons were cruelly clamped around my ankles to augment the handcuffs.

Reaching the prison, I hobbled between the policemen to a desk where an officer sat. "This is the dastardly Lord Durham, is it?" His voice sounded like ice cracking on a frozen river. Pulling documents from a drawer, he began to read.

Colonel Hathaway, Chief Constable of the Durham County Constabulary, had not been idle. He'd sent a warrant for my arrest to every conceivable location where I might be apprehended.

The warrant was accompanied by a complete dossier of relevant facts, including a complete physical description. This, I later learned, was provided by Marjorie. I would remain in the jail until an escort could be summoned from England, possibly three or four months.

If I had leprosy, I doubt I'd be more isolated. Not one of my friends, including Mary, paid me a visit although my incarceration was front-page news.

Ghastly days of fear dragged by in the gloom of my Spartan cell, terrifying thoughts my only companions. With relief, guards removed me from my cell one morning and placed me in the custody of two stalwarts of the Durham County Constabulary.

The long land journey to Halifax completed, we boarded the vessel taking me back to England. Strangely, the voyage was far more comfortable than my trip to Canada. My escorts and I travelled cabin class. We ate well, had comfortable quarters and could enjoy the view of the ocean.

The leg irons remained in place and one of the constables guarded me day and night. They weren't unpleasant, asking many questions about the events of Stella's death and my escape from Colonel Hathaway. This accomplishment seemed to amuse them.

England of memory a green and pleasant land, was cold, gray and miserable. My trial would be held in Manchester, so we proceeded directly there after docking.

Entering the familiar streets, I remembered so many years of my learning process in the employment of my father. Stronger still were memories of Stella. After nearly two months of travel, I said goodbye to my escort as I was taken to my cell, an older, dirtier, urine-smelling replica of the one in Toronto.

In three weeks the trial began before Judge Stephen, the most famous judge in England, who had presided over every sensational case I remembered. He was an austere, wizened figure of a man, whose cutting remarks sliced through rhetoric as easily as a broom clears cobwebs.

My barrister, an overbearing and pompous ass, pleaded my defense as temporary insanity. Finding my lover unfaithful, he cajoled, was all it took to snap my power of reasoning.

The Crown Attorney did a devastating job in picturing me as a wanton, unfaithful husband, who, with wealth, power and prestige, chose a road of lust and deceit ending in cold-blooded murder.

Substantiating his evidence, he produced some of my ex-servants, including Hull, who verified every fact. Stella's life was thoroughly investigated as well, for, brought to the witness stand were two leading lights of the Methodist Church Charity Brigade. These two told of the dedication and love Stella showed to all in need.

Marjorie made a brief appearance to state, in a clear, unwavering voice, that she'd been aware of my unfaithfulness. She'd done nothing for the sake of the children and the family name.

After such damning testimony, it was a relief when the verdict came and sentence was passed: "to be hanged by the neck until dead." The words had long since lost their terror as I knew their inevitability. The ordeal of being a public spectacle was finished. The next public appearance would be brief with only a clergyman, the prison governor and the hangman present.

CHAPTER 38

Poverty and the Preachers

Christened Natasha, I'm the youngest daughter of Steven and Tania Korkov. From birth I knew my mother hated me for, as the nurse gently handed me to her after my first breaths, she called in anguish for someone to take away the deformed baby.

The last thing mother wanted was another child. My two older brothers she tolerated; they were useful around the miserable quarter section of land from which we tried to scratch a living.

My three sisters, born after the boys, accepted life as a dreary experience without affection, filled with constant chores and hungry bellies. My sickly health, withered arm and leg, did nothing to produce the sympathetic understanding that may have been expected.

My brothers and sisters loathed my constant crying, that they knew by experience would infuriate both parents. From the day of my birth, I think, I knew I was a burden to all.

The Korkov's house consisted of four rooms. A kitchen was crowded with a black wood-burning stove, four chairs and a rough hewn table resting on two saw horses. There was a bedroom for the boys, practically filled by their brass bedstead and the few clothes hung on nails.

In another room, no larger, we girls all shared the same dilapidated bed. The fourth room served two purposes. It was the storeroom for food and contained a large galvanized tub for all laundry, dishes and personal ablutions.

The unpainted structure was built of clapboard and odd pieces of wood. Knotholes were stuffed with rags to reduce the drafts. Defecation or urination took place in a stinking outhouse a hundred feet north. The only other structure on the property was a decaying barn.

I can only guess how different my parents would have been if their wishes had come true. In the old country, the promised emigration held out the hope of entering a land of plenty. Instead, they scratched a meager subsistence from a desert, baking in summer, freezing all winter.

The harshness seeped into their souls, driving youth and dreams into oblivion. Replacing it was a sustained anger at a situation from which there was no escape.

Before reaching my first birthday, I sustained many blackened eyes and nosebleeds from mother's hand. She knew if she didn't discipline me, my father would attack her in an equally brutal fashion.

The house sweltered in heat in summer and literally froze in winter. The only heat provided was by the black stove, filled with fast-burning poplar. My parents slept on a mattress they placed on the table in the kitchen when ready for bed.

Until I was too large, my cradle was the washtub with an old blanket folded as a mattress. When dishes or washing was to be done, they lifted me in my blanket, placing me in some temporary place.

As my parents spoke no English, they had little social contact with our neighbors scattered like tiny oases in this vast, flat land. We children were better off, as it was compulsory to send us to school.

Mrs. Jorgansen, our buxom teacher, filled our life with stories of distant places while teaching us to read and write. The teasing about my arm and leg by fellow students rarely stopped. The twice-a-day five mile journey was torturous, but the respite from home was worth every step and indignity.

I survived; we all did. One of my brothers took a job on a larger farm when he was able. The eldest decided to stay and help Father who, by this time, was in failing health.

My sisters drifted away, one to marry a local boy, another to work as a waitress in a large city. The youngest, next to me, found work in a store. Mother said they could be stuck with me for life. Although I was pretty, nobody would want to marry or employ a cripple, she explained. I decided then to show her she was wrong.

The advertisement in *The Liberty Chronicle* read, "Christian family requires housekeeper of same persuasion. Must be clean, neat and hard worker. Must enjoy children. Duties include: cooking, cleaning, child care. Fair wages, security and comfortable, private quarters. One day off a week after proving worth and dedication. Apply in person to: Reverend Peter Spanks, Minot Full Evangelical Church Rectory, 11 Railway Street, Minot, North Dakota."

The following day, on the pretext that I must buy something of a personal nature from the druggist in town, I walked ten miles to Stanton. I carried a box of clothing I'd hidden in the barn the previous night. I went immediately to the railroad station.

Although frightened, I paid the fare to Minot, leaving me less than a dollar. I spent all the money I possessed — twenty-six dollars and thirty cents, accumulated over ten years. Chores for neighbors, a gift from a sister and brother at Christmas, four dollars found outside a bar. I had secreted the money under a board in the outhouse.

I liked the Reverend Spanks at first sight. He ushered me into a plush office with overstuffed chairs, a chesterfield and glowing lamps. He was tall and handsome, with bright brown eyes and a shock of fair hair hanging over his forehead.

His wife, also tall and brown eyed, I heard speak sharply when the maid announced me, "Just another slut who will help fill the void of this worldly life."

A slamming of a door muffled some other remarks she made. I heard enough to get the meaning: while he advised others to wait patiently for paradise, he sought it in every pretty face and figure. I didn't like her. If these remarks were directed at him, Reverend Spanks didn't show anger. After a brief interview, he said I'd fit nicely into the position he offered.

He stipulated, however, that his dear wife, Mrs. Spanks, must make the final judgment. Opening a door, he summoned his wife in soft but commanding tones. Mrs. Spanks, sulking, entered the room casting accusing eyes in my direction. I rose fearfully, knowing her opinion of me would decide my fate.

Her eyes swept from my face to my feet, feasting I thought, with pleasure, on my withered arm and shorter leg that caused me to list to one side.

She asked about my background and my beliefs. I answered truthfully. My religion was not of her persuasion. I'd been raised Greek Orthodox. I hadn't attended church, I added, as the only churches close were Protestant and Roman Catholic.

She sniffed by way of reply, saying I would do if I proved myself during a probation period. She sourly added, as I was young, there was still time to lead me to Jesus.

My living quarters consisted of a small room in the basement containing a bed, dresser, water jug, basin and a wooden chair. Above the bed hung a large painting of Jesus. I was delighted; never had I enjoyed such comfortable quarters. The bed had a huge eiderdown stuffed with goose feathers. More luxurious were the glistening white sheets.

Another person resided in the basement, Tom Jackson. He was a bit older than me and had a room similar to mine on the other side of the basement. When Reverend Spanks introduced us, he hung his head, more interested in his foot drawing patterns on the concrete floor.

Tom is the handyman, the Reverend explained, doing everything from cutting the grass to cleaning the church. Dismissing Tom to his duties, the Reverend explained that Tom was slow-witted.

"He does a good job once he gets the hang of it. We employ him as he is a creation of God, like us. It is our duty to protect all His flock." My duties started at six in the morning, often continuing until late evening. I liked the young Spanks children, Emily and Justin, a feeling they reciprocated, to the resentment of their mother.

Life was good, consistent with the benefits listed in the advertisement I answered. However, six or seven weeks after I started work, an event occurred that would be my downfall.

Tom and Mrs. Spanks were out of the house. Mrs. Spanks was doing the weekly shopping; Tom was engaged in his usual chores in the church. I walked into the office to clean. Surprised, I saw Mr. Spanks, whom I thought out also, hard at work at his desk.

He looked up smiling, "Sermons are a never-ending battle. Trying to develop new ideas to maintain interest is a difficult task." Placing his pen on the papers, he stretched, saying we should talk.

"Sit, Natasha," he said, suggesting the couch. He questioned me about my childhood, our poor farm, my family. He had a knack of digging into my deepest emotions.

At first I'd been happy to talk. As he pressed deeper, tears flooded my eyes, running down my cheeks. I talked of things never divulged: my dreams, fears and frustrations. The scars I so carefully shielded about being crippled were exposed to the light by his gentle probing.

My agitation grew; so did his sympathy and understanding. He sat beside me, gently wiping away my tears with his handkerchief. He said not to cry; I had much for which to rejoice.

Jesus loved me, and, although my leg and arm may be crippled, my magnificent beauty of face and figure more than compensated for the flaws. He held me, stroking my hair.

Never had I experienced this loving tenderness. My father never touched me other than to cuff me when I displeased him. The times Mother had shown affection could be counted on my thumbs. My brothers, sisters and I, always so confined together, developed an idea that bliss was being alone.

"Do you like me holding you like this?" the Reverend whispered. I nodded. "Then we must talk again, Natasha. I think you're a wonderful, beautiful young woman."

His tender caring thrilled me. Deep within, something stirred, something which could be called desire. I was now seventeen. I had never been with a man except in my dreams. My imagination was rooted in a past era, maidens being rescued by knights riding white horses. I hoped the Reverend would again open this new world of flowing emotions. However, it wasn't Reverend Spanks who next professed his admiration for me; it was poor Tom Jackson. Tom approached me shyly in the basement as I was going to bed. He whispered in the shadows, outside the radius of my lantern's glow.

He wanted to speak to me, asking if I would mind. I smiled, holding the light higher and inviting Tom, who looked like a startled deer, to come closer. In an eager shuffling gait, he did.

"I love you, Natasha," he whispered in a hoarse voice. Before I could speak, he grabbed my hand, put it to his lips, kissing it hard. Then he retreated into the darkness toward his room.

I felt amazed and flattered by his actions. I scarcely knew Tom although sharing the basement with him. I talked to him, of course, having once brought him hot soup when he was ill.

I liked Tom as a little boy, for although he was large and muscular, his manner belied his maturity. Tom, I judged, had the mental capacity of a child of ten, although I'd been told he was twenty six.

Mrs. Spanks, however, was a different matter. I disliked her, although she, at rare intervals, could be pleasant. Usually she was cold and demanding, expecting much and giving little.

Her relationship with the Reverend puzzled me. With others around, she was the adoring wife. When alone, the adoration extinguished like a snuffed candle. Her eyes followed him distrustfully, reminding me of a dog having been kicked by its master.

I enjoyed church, being privileged to sit near the front where I had a good view of the proceedings. The Reverend sparkled in his pulpit. Sometimes his voice thundered as he waved an accusing finger at his congregation. At other times he sounded close to tears, his voice low and subdued.

Often he looked heavenward, or so it seemed, claiming he could see God and His angels watching over us. At times, his robes rustling, his hands accentuating what he voiced, he seemed a reflection of the God he worshiped. His urging to "Do unto others as we would have done unto us" filled my heart. I wished to give him the love and kindness he gave me. In a way, I worshiped him.

CHAPTER 39

Sinister Seduction

I helped Mrs. Spanks carry her bags to the front door. The Reverend then drove her in his buggy to the station. She planned to be away for a week, visiting her ailing mother. It didn't take long for the Reverend to take advantage of her absence.

After lunch, the Reverend suggested I visit him in his office to continue the talk we had last week. I responded with pleasure that after finishing the dishes and other chores, I'd come.

Quickly I finished my work, then on impulse, went to my room to put on my prettiest dress and comb my hair. Since my arrival, I'd worn my hair in a tight bun, now it cascaded free to the small of my back. With excited anticipation, I knocked on the office door.

The Reverend gasped. Never had he seen me dressed like this, nor my hair in its natural state. I knew Mrs. Spanks would have heartily disapproved had she been present. "Natasha, you look beautiful, like an angel," said the Reverend in admiration.

Taking my hand, he suggested I should sit on the couch. Immediately he continued the topic we'd been discussing almost a week ago. It was like there had merely been a pause in the conversation.

Again shadows of the past illuminated, tears flooding my eyes. He sat beside me with his strong arms drawing me to his understanding warmth.

I don't know how it happened, but it did. My head felt light, any sense of propriety vanished, a feeling of need engulfed my reason. I was aflame with a passion only the Reverend could extinguish.

Gentle fingers probed and stroked, making me delirious with want. I could scarcely breathe, the feeling was so excruciating. There was no need of his help in removing my clothes; I was more than willing. Then he took off his pants.

We lay together damp and breathless. Slowly the passion ebbed although, I knew, if he started again, I'd be pleased.

The reverie was shattered as the chimes of the little clock in its glass and brass case tolled the hour. "Goodness!" he said, dislodging himself from my arms. "The Johnsons will be here in ten minutes."

We met every afternoon Mrs. Spanks was away. Guilt gnawed at my innards. When I mentioned it to him, he dismissed my feelings by telling me of his plight.

Mrs. Spanks denied him what was rightfully his as a husband. This was wrong, he said, quoting the Bible about becoming one flesh in marriage. He said he loved me. I replied I loved him as well.

"Then we must continue to love one another," he replied. "Unfortunately, it must be hidden. Mrs. Spanks must never discover our little secret, must she?" I understood.

Peter (he'd asked me to call him by his first name in private) and I took every opportunity to consummate our love. When Mrs. Spanks went out, we used the office; sometimes, in the dead of night, Peter slipped silently into my room. This wasn't difficult as he and his wife had separate bedrooms.

Six months later I missed my period. I didn't become alarmed at first but as weeks turned to months, I was aware life was developing within me. Then I felt fear.

I trusted Peter to protect me; I could depend on him. I waited for Tuesday, Mrs. Spanks' shopping day. I'd tell him then. No longer was preliminary talk necessary. When I entered the office, Peter was ready for the pleasure we shared.

But this afternoon I wanted to talk, so I resisted his attempts to unbutton my clothing. A cloud darkened his expression. "Come on, Natasha," he said impatiently. "She won't be long, and it has been four days, you realize?"

His irritability shocked me. Never before had he exhibited such behavior. I stuck to my guns. "We must talk, Peter. It's very important."

Quickly, the words tumbling over each other, I told him I was pregnant. The silence was profound. He said nothing; the only sound was the faint ticking of the desk-top clock. I wondered if he'd understood. His expression said he had.

His face paled, his eyes stared at my belly as if it were Satan himself. "Peter," I said softly, extending my hand.

He thrust it aside savagely, his lips curved into a grimace of pain. "You bitch. How could you be so stupid?"

He thrust me toward the door. "Get your things packed right now and get out of here immediately, do you understand? At once! Before my wife comes home. You're fired, finished, out!"

I stumbled my way to the basement room that minutes before had been secure, my sanctuary, my space of refuge in a huge, cold world. Through stinging tears I pulled my suitcase from under the bed.

Opening it, I began stuffing my personal effects from the chest of drawers. I was in a nightmare; everything seemed unreal. Just minutes before life had been happy, complete. Now fate swept down an icy gorge, taking me away from everything I cherished.

I swirled through the mechanical motions of placing my things in my suitcase. Only a few minutes had passed, I suppose, for I was in such a state of misery, time meant nothing.

Somebody rushed downstairs and flung the door of my room open. Peter, appearing red-faced and furious, yelled, "Get out, get out! What is keeping you?" He crammed the last of my belongings from the drawer into the suitcase.

I tried to speak through my constricted throat. I failed. The only sounds I made were rasping sobs. This inflamed his anger to greater velocity. Grabbing my shoulder, he threw me against the wall, checked the drawers, then snapped the suitcase shut.

He turned to me, yanking me behind him toward the door. My ankle buckled, sending me crashing to the floor. "For Christ's sake, get up girl!" he thundered, slapping me hard across the face. Everything became a blur. The Reverend's face seemed to disintegrate into a shower of spurting blood. One of his eyes popped out of its socket. I rolled to one side as his body crashed to the floor beside me.

Behind the Reverend stood Tom, a bloodied hammer still in his hand. He half grinned, "He won't be hurtin' you any more, Natasha."

Everything spun crazily in a slow moving circle. Somebody else entered the room . . . a woman . . . I could see shoes and skirts. Ear-splitting screams intensified the madness. Mrs. Spanks discovered her husband's body twitching in the throes of death.

"You've killed him! You've murdered my husband!" she screamed, her voice shrilling louder. Again Tom swung the hammer. Mrs. Spanks fell across her husband's body like a shot mallard. Her limp arm cradled him in a farewell of death.

I can scarcely remember what happened then: Tom half carrying me up the stairs and out of the house, scrambling with Tom's strong arm pulling me . . . down railroad tracks into a dark shed.

Outside, something hissed and screeched. The shed shuddered, the sounds of a hammer hitting metal, the smell of smoke in the air. As my head cleared, I strained my eyes to see where we were.

The enclosure I'd thought was a shed turned out to be an empty boxcar. Tom's simple face looked into mine. "Don't worry, Natasha. We'll soon be out of here," he whispered, running his calloused hand roughly over my cheek.

I was too numb to think or act. The dreadful incidents replayed in my memory, a symphony composed in hell. Peter's cold rejection and hostility, his face disintegrating, his eye oozing from its socket, hanging down his face, Mrs. Spank's hysterical screams, her silent embrace of death.

Vaguely, I was aware of our boxcar moving, jolting backward, stopping momentarily, then proceeding forward to a quickening sound of clicking wheels. "You see, Natasha, we'll be miles from here soon," yelled Tom above the accelerating rattle of the train. Dazed, frightened, the horror of the events in the rectory so overpowering, I couldn't pull my thoughts together. I realized I was travelling toward an unknown destination with a man who'd committed two murders.

There was no fear of Tom within me, for I trusted the gentleness he'd always shown me. The train began losing speed, the lights of some town blinked coldly in the darkness through the crack in the partially opened door. We stopped, metal grinding against metal. Tom slid the door closed.

Two sounds predominated. One was the sound of someone rapping the wheels of the train with a hammer. The other, the sound of men's voices and the opening and slamming of doors. Tom pulled me gently into the farthest corner of the boxcar.

The voices became more distinct as the men moved closer. "Nothing in here. Try the next one." The crunch of footsteps stopped outside; our door opened wide; a lantern's beam glowed, encircled our sanctuary and stopped on us. A voice cried in triumph, "They're here boys. We've got 'em."

We spent a horrendous night in adjoining cells, leered at by cigar-smoking men. The following day we returned to Minot, with four sheriff's deputies as escorts. A waiting throng of citizens howled, "String 'em up."

During my trial I told the absolute truth, as I had sworn to do on the Bible. It did no good. The prosecutor wove a tale of dementia, saying Tom and I were lovers.

Both of us, he suggested, a cripple and a simpleton, were hired by the good Reverend and his lamented wife through the goodness of their hearts as they helped the less fortunate.

We returned this favor by brutally murdering them. The Reverend Spanks and his wife, he suggested, had perhaps discovered us in the act of copulation. During their admonition of our sinful conduct, we had killed them both.

My defense attorney, who I was sure never believed my story, did his best. He pointed out that Tom had admitted killing both the Spankses, absolving me of any part of the blame.

It was useless. Found guilty as an accessory to the crime, I was sentenced to be hanged.

As I was being escorted to the gallows, I had the strangest feeling this was a replay of an old nightmare. It had, in some distant past, happened before. The clergyman said some prayers and spoke of a forgiving God.

With a hood shutting out the world around me, I waited for the floor to disappear under my feet, a rope's length to eternity. Knowing I was innocent, that God knew the truth, I wasn't afraid.

CHAPTER 40

Loose Ends

Instead of a cruel jerk snapping my neck, I opened my eyes to Samantha's lovely face. It resembled waking from a nightmare, only better as nightmares are reserved for the earthly state. Here, unless reliving a lifetime, there was no such thing, or so I believed.

"Boy, I can really blow a good thing, can't I?" It was a statement, not a question, but Samantha addressed it anyway. "We all can. Sometimes we're given every opportunity to be successful, to do something for our fellow beings, then the lust for personal gain and power interferes."

"Those three lifetimes were interrelated for a purpose, I suppose?" I asked, sure the deduction forming in my mind was correct. Samantha smiled the radiance of eternity, her energy waves merging with mine.

"You know the answer, Richard. Each lifetime presents an opportunity for spiritual growth. Sometimes you advanced, sometimes you didn't."

She grimaced. "You realize, I shouldn't be calling you Richard. It's the particular name you obtained during your last incarnation. You are no more Richard than you are Siba, Sinta's daughter. Nor should I call you by any other earthly names or titles you once used — Rebecca, George, Gerhard, Your Worship or Your Lordship, for instance."

I grinned. The idea of Samantha calling me "Your Worship" was ludicrous. Samantha read my mind. "When you were entitled to being addressed in that manner, you wouldn't have been amused if it hadn't been used, would you? It was important to you then, as were all the baubles of earthly life.

"It is only those advanced souls nearing completion of their earthly spiral, who can clearly differentiate. They know what is valuable for their soul's progress, as opposed to the temporal gains of the earth cycle."

"Explain how some of the lifetimes I experienced were interconnected, will you?" I asked. "And how I advanced or failed." Samantha nodded.

"In Atlantis you advanced spiritually for good reason. In a society that treated drones as genetically engineered slaves, you showed compassion for Sinta, putting your job and social standing at risk. Your indoctrination and training meant less than the feelings you felt. God's reflection within you gave you compassion and love.

"As Rebecca, you had a chance to give loyalty and devotion to a courageous husband. You failed because you couldn't give up comforts of the flesh. Position and money meant more to you than did Abram.

"As a Cardinal in the Church, not only did you reimpose the Indulgences you knew to be morally wrong, but you lusted for, and then corrupted a young woman, leading to her suicide.

"Your dreadful life as a slave tried to teach you the agony of those subjected to the tyranny of others. You lacked a choice. You were forced to work, suffer and obey.

"As George Humphrey you had a marvelous opportunity to help the poor and underprivileged. At first you understood the plight of the working class. Then your ideals disintegrated in the pursuit of personal vanity, power and lust.

"You chose the disadvantaged life of Natasha hoping it would teach you humility and an understanding for the less fortunate. It was regrettable your path led you to Reverend Spanks, as you were young, trusting and vulnerable to his advances. Again, sensuality led to your downfall. For you knew, deep within, that what you did was wrong."

I nodded in agreement. I knew. I realized my life as Natasha had been useful as one salient lesson etched itself in my subconscious. Every person's actions, good or bad, large or small, affected those around him.

I felt the greatest shame knowing how depraved I'd become as George Humphrey, and said so. Samantha took my hand. "Many souls do things equally bad, sometimes much worse. It's true you murdered, ended the lifetime of two bodies, but you know now that there is no such thing as death.

"Not that I'm trying to reduce the severity of what you did; I'm not. Still, you didn't premeditate murder. It resulted from your passion and greed. What I'm comparing it with are the crimes committed in the name of national pride, the creation of money, the usurping of power for power's sake. Crimes that have plunged millions into war and poverty."

She agreed my life as George Humphrey offered an outstanding opportunity to advance myself spiritually. Unfortunately, while beginning with great promise, I deteriorated into a tyrannical despot who cared for nothing except my own gratification.

I felt deep concern for the others who shared these lifetimes. For instance, had Stella and Marjorie also been involved during my short tragic life as Natasha?

The joy of creation echoed in her laughter. "You are beginning to be knowledgeable in the dynamics of our creations. Yes, of course, those two souls with whom you have spent so many bodily years were present.

"Realizing their bonding with you left many problems to be resolved, they chose to enter the flesh in the same period. In this way, they hoped those problems would be brought to a satisfactory conclusion.

"They, as well, had lessons to learn that could elevate them in the spiritual world. Marjorie, humiliated and disgraced by your actions when married to you, wished to rid herself of the desire to seek revenge.

"She chose to be a man in a following life and, following her inclination of ridding herself of anger and revenge, became a clergyman. You turned to this clergyman for the love and understanding you needed as a wretched young woman, physically and mentally abused.

"You craved a mature and understanding paternal love. Unfortunately, to use your expression, she blew it. She had the most wonderful opportunity of helping others in that life. Not only you, as Natasha, but many who entered her life when she was Peter Spanks.

"Can you think of another person involved with you as Richard Nelson that could have been involved in your life as George Humphrey?" I thought hard. There were Mother and Father, of course. Their treatment of me could be warranted if they were among the people I'd hurt over many lifetimes. I rejected this. Karma doesn't work this way. Souls don't enter the world for revenge.

Involved, having a bearing on events? My mind raced back. Could it be Mrs. Jorgansen, I wondered? She was a glow of light in a sea of misery. Or, could it possibly be Tom?

It was Tom, for Tom was the one so directly involved in the termination of my life as Natasha. Poor Tom, a decent and kindly person whose love for me as Natasha was the catalyst in ending both our lives.

I asked Samantha if this was correct. She nodded, explaining the soul who'd chosen to enter Tom's body was none other than my father, Sir Hubert Humphrey. From knowledge gained in the spiritual state, he realized he needed the lesson of humility. He'd therefore chosen to become a person with impaired mental abilities.

"Fate brought us together?" I asked. "You know better than that," she laughed. "The Creator makes possible many situations to help us in bodily form. As you will remember, the outcome is left entirely to our free will."

I felt a vague sense of understanding the vastness of the great plan of life. Clear comprehension still belonged in a dimension beyond my grasp. In an explosive insight, I was aware of the panorama of life existing as one grain of sand amongst trillions.

The grain of sand was the earth upon which we lived — we and uncounted trillions of insects, animals, birds, reptiles and fish. Within these untold, unfathomable other existences were microorganisms, viruses, bacteria — worlds within worlds.

Life, death and always rebirth. Everything constantly changing form and physical appearance, yet changeless in essence. The identical building blocks for everything that breathes. The same building blocks creating inanimate objects.

Intelligence as a part of all living species, trees being able to communicate danger by producing a particular scent, water scientifically proven to have some form of memory.

Earthly time rushing by in human eyes, yet everything happening simultaneously. Perhaps this earth drama was happening in all the galaxies. Life, death, rebirth, all presided over by a Creative Force of unimaginable power and grandeur.

A Force, from the human perspective, visible only in the eyes of a child, or, in acts of kindness, the courage of a dog saving its drowning master, great music, the beauty of nature and above all, the love of one for another.

I surrendered myself to a breathtakingly serene humility. My lust, savagery, dishonesty, pomposity, untruthfulness, hatefulness and so many other defects in my spiritual character were surely causes for annihilation. Yet, that great Creator with the patience of infinity provided the schooling, leading me eventually into His Light.

I am a speck in space, living on a larger speck, the little Earth floating among the billions of planets. Yet the Creator allows me my follies as I am His creation, a part of Him.

Samantha read my thoughts as if they'd been displayed on a printed page. She held me in her radiant love before speaking. "To the extent of your capability, you've glimpsed the essence of the Truth.

"As God has created us, we are, therefore, part of Him. It is similar to a great composer of music, a great painter or writer: once the work is complete, the work stands on its own. Yet, I believe you'll agree that a part of whoever created that particular work remains in the creation.

"You can't hear the music of Mozart, Chopin or Bach, for instance, without sensing the talent and genius of those who created it. It is the same with the work of a Michaelangelo or a Shakespeare. Part of their genius will always remain alive in their creation.

"What I'm saying, Richard, as I've said so often before, is that the Creator does not abandon His work, no matter how many twisted turns it might take, for the Creator lives in His creation."

I digested this, knowing she'd made the point before in a different way. Again, my earthly religious upbringing seemed to impinge upon her logic, my memory regurgitating the warnings of hell and damnation.

Samantha sighed. "It's strange how fear dominates our feelings and emotions. This is an issue we always have to deal with as it's ingrained into a soul's memory.

"Remember, each generation on earth is living in the present. Religious leaders believe it is their duty to advance their flocks spiritually. They find the greatest tool in their arsenal is fear. It's like telling children they'll get punished if they do wrong. In your religion's case, the punishment is more severe — hell and eternal damnation.

"They tell believers they have a loving God, then turn around and say, irrespective of the circumstances, it's the last chance. Fail in this life and you'll pay the price in eternity.

"They're right, to a point. Punishment is given for sins. We must pay the price of rectifying that sin. This knowledge could be as much a deterrent as is the other cruel assertion of only one chance if only they viewed a lifetime as it is — one brief chapter in a long book."

There remained a point that wasn't clear, so I asked Samantha. "Are some souls incorrigible, beyond any hope of redemption?" The question produced a grave expression before Samantha answered. "I really don't know. I can't speak for God, nor do I know the Creator's mind.

"There is something I haven't shown you. I doubted you were ready. I thought during your next visit here we'd have a look. Perhaps you're ready for a short tour now." She held my hand. In an instant, we were in a brightly lit bar. The bar wasn't unusual; I'd been in some practically identical.

People were enjoying themselves, the sounds of conversation, and laughter blending with music. What is the point? I wondered. It was nothing new.

A film formed over my eyes, then cleared, revealing the forms of people I hadn't previously noticed. I use the word "forms" as this is what they were. Obviously, they weren't flesh and blood, for they were opaque, light on the extremities, becoming darker on the inside.

They moved among the real people unobserved, trying to draw attention to themselves. Some appeared to have blank expressions; others displayed the characteristics of evil. These grasped at patrons with vaporous hands.

"These souls are those who refuse to proceed toward the light of the Creator. They're found everywhere mankind lives, in bars, in business establishments, in government offices, in religious organizations, anywhere of interest to them.

"Some are merely unfortunate, others are the embodiment of evil. Instead of sticking to the Creator's plan of spiritual advancement, they become power-hungry, taking pleasure in the manipulation of mankind for their dark purposes.

"They retain considerable power, usurping it, trying to influence people to follow their malevolent ways. Their greatest assets are the character flaws in their intendend victims: pride, greed, lust, power, vanity.

"We work on the unfortunate souls — in some ways we resemble Stella's Charity Brigade. We try to steer them to the light of true understanding. The others, the very evil beings, turn their backs on us.

"Perhaps they believe they have the power of God. I don't know what the Creator will eventually do about them. They could be destroyed in a second, if God so wished."

CHAPTER 41

Body Bound

Gradually I became aware that my time of instruction could be finished. Recently, Sonia said goodbye to resume a bodily life, saying she dreaded the return but realized it necessary for her spiritual education.

She had a feeling she'd do better this time, making headway toward freeing herself of the cycle of birth and death. I missed her, of course, but it wasn't the same as an earthly death of a loved one. I knew she lived and thought we'd be reunited.

Around Sonia's time of departure, Mrs. Dunne and Duncan Watson said goodbye. I got a real jolt from Major MacDougal, for he intended a return to earth life immediately. He hadn't changed, retaining his booming voice and sense of humor.

Jokingly, he said he wanted to get back to the flesh before me to ensure he'd always be a step ahead. Then he became serious, saying how much he'd learned, how desperately he wished to graduate to the highest levels.

We were all wiser, I knew, but as this had happened before after each earthly death, how much knowledge we would retain? I wished him well, saying I hoped we'd meet again.

Samantha lovingly confirmed I was again ready to enter another lifetime. I would miss her more than anybody. Her love was all embracing and demanded nothing. I mentioned this and she replied she was merely like the moon, reflecting the greater love of the Creative Force.

Although feeling ready to progress to bodily life, I still had a multitude of unanswered questions. Samantha explained many would have to wait until I evolved to a higher plane. She herself would have to evolve before being granted more knowledge. She confirmed some intuitions I felt. Sinta, the lovely young woman engineered as a drone, bore me as her daughter, Siba, but Sinta herself became entwined with me again over time as Simone and then Sonia.

Thyrza, my friend in the time of Jesus, became my mother when I was Gerhard, a German soldier killed in World War I.

I became frightened as the time approached to don flesh. I knew the hard, cruel, often bitter existence I must face. I remembered there were times of love and tenderness, joy and happiness, excitement, failure, exhilaration, crushing sadness and abject misery.

I realized that for a brief instant after birth I would remember the purpose of my journey. Then, as if a blindfold was placed on the eyes of memory, all recollection of spiritual enlightenment would vanish like the sun behind a cloud.

Possibly, if I'd learned enough, an occasional, brilliant flash of insight would brighten my journey by realizing its purpose. I hoped so; the life I'd helped select would be difficult.

It would be a life without personal vanity or the pursuit of wealth and power, a lifetime to try to master the devil of the flesh, my ego. I would be a naked infant soon, setting out on the journey that leads to a greater life through physical death.

CHAPTER 42

Born Again

My warm world shattered in a torrent of dreadful convulsions.

Inexplicably, relentlessly I'm pushed by the agony of contractions toward the harsh reality of cold and light. The wonderful, soft voice that spoke so lovingly to me, now gasped in pain.

I'm rejected, thrust away from my sheltering home, squeezed ever tighter, forced protesting through shuddering canyon walls, the slow, methodical rhythm of love now a racing torment, a thundering drum of sound. Am I to be destroyed?

Now I'm free, turned upside down and hit, placed on something both hard and soft, to be examined and wiped clean. The memory shines like a shooting star as I feel the soft breast of my loving mother.

"Welcome to the world, Richard darling." Before the darkness returns, just for a split second, I realize Sonia and I again face life together.

I'd begun the journey chosen with the help of Samantha and other Guides. I wasn't aware of the concern I caused. Doctors shook their heads in futility as they examined me.

"He's grotesque," said one nurse. Another offered an opinion it might be kinder to let me die through neglect. The attending physician, delicately suggesting this option to my mother, received an angry response.

Condemnation of the medical staff involved would be unfair. They hadn't knowledge of the master plan suggested by the Guides. Nor, consciously, did my mother.

In the "Halfway House" she'd given her assent to the drastic measure after deep discussions with the Guides. It would be a difficult challenge, they said, but one offering great potential for benefiting our souls' evolution.

Both souls, Sonia's and mine, had faltered in other earthly lives because of lusts of the flesh. When faced with great opportunities to advance spiritually, we often succumbed to earthly attachments.

We both searched for happiness in the illusions of carnal pleasures, in power and prestige. Neither of us realized that what we so frantically sought we already possessed. For deep within us was the bliss of eternity, the loving essence of God. Unfortunately, I'd usually been the instigator of our road to ruin.

I lived due to my mother's love. All we possessed, two years after my birth, was each other. My father, insisting he place me in an institution, left my mother when she refused his demand.

Most people considered our lives wretched. We lived in two small rooms and shared a stinking communal bathroom. Mother made her living by working at night, cleaning expensive, often luxurious offices.

A portion of her inadequate wage was spent providing nightcare for me. Her youthful attractiveness soon faded. Lined and haggard, she merged into the nameless multitude of shadowy, night-working people, whose menial task was to ensure the comfort and cleanliness of prestigious offices.

She didn't complain. As years passed, she maintained a deep inner sense that what she was doing was right. Her love permeated through the dullness of my mind, filling me with a radiance of well-being. She was the channel of God, pouring forth inexhaustible currents of love to fill and brighten my life.

Scrimping on her most basic needs, she purchased art supplies as she thought I might enjoy dabbing colors on the paper. To her amazement, I drew a picture that resembled a large, Tudor- style home.

In quick succession I also drew or painted other objects she thought remarkable: a space vehicle, a scene Mother thought resembled the Holy Land, then a cathedral, to be followed by a realistic-looking battle scene from World War II.

Mother became dumbfounded and frightened. Since birth, eleven years ago, I'd accomplished nothing. Often, the most simple functions of life, such as eating with cutlery or washing myself, taxed my abilities.

Thanks to a charitable organization which paid the costs, I attended a medical clinic once a month for medical assessment. Mother, perplexed, but delighted by my new-found acuity in art, took along a sample of my work to show the doctor.

His first reaction in examining my work was one of incredulity. Then, convinced by mother this work was mine, he asked if he might borrow it for awhile.

A month passed before we again entered the clinic. To mother's surprise, two other men were with the doctor — one, a noted brain specialist, the other the curator of the art section of a large museum.

According to them, my pictures aroused great interest in both the medical and art world. It wasn't because of their technical excellence, but the scenes portrayed.

"For instance," said the curator of the museum, "Richard's picture depicting a World War II battle was obvious authenticity. We took it to an historian who is expert in all phases of military history. He became convinced the troops shown were Canadian by their uniforms, shoulder patches and weapons.

"Not being content with his assessment, he took the battle scene drawing to the Military Archives in Ottawa, Canada. It was examined by leading military historians who, without hesitation, gave their opinion it depicted a bloody battle the Canadian Second Division fought in Belgium during 1944.

"That isn't the most incredible part. The incomprehensible fact is that Richard sketched a small crest in the lower, left-hand portion of the picture," he pointed his finger. "That crest accurately depicts the badge of a regiment involved, The Calgary Highlanders."

The brain specialist entered the conversation. "Richard has always lived in New York, hasn't he?" Mother said yes. "He can't read, can he, and has never been particularly interested in books?" Mother replied it was true.

"Have you any reference material concerning the Second World War in your home, or could Richard have had access to any such material?" Mother shook her head.

"We have one of these perplexing problems that confound us," said the brain specialist. "Richard shouldn't have the knowledge or the capability to depict such events. He does." The curator interrupted, "There is more to relate. The cathedral picture, experts say, contains all the architectural features authentically. These are things even a skilled artist might exclude."

Excitedly, Mother asked if this meant I was improving. Did it mean my brain was beginning to function normally? Sadly, the brain specialist shook his head. "I'm afraid not. What Richard's talents show is that he is what we call an idiot savant — a mentally defective person who exhibits exceptional skill in one field.

"Where he gets his knowledge is beyond any of us." He laughed, "Have you ever heard of reincarnation?" "I've heard of it, yes," replied mother, "but I don't know a thing about it."

The brain specialist smiled. "Neither do I. But there are so many inexplicable aspects to human consciousness, such as Richard's talent. Near-death experiences suggest a continuation of awareness after bodily death. Psychic phenomena point to human capacities barely developed in most of us.

"Some well-investigated studies using hypnosis and historical investigation showed that some people know, in great detail, the life and times of a person far removed from the present. And," he continued, "there are hundreds of authentic cases, meticulously investigated, of young children claiming to have lived as another person in a recent lifetime.

"Sometimes, leading scientific investigators can authenticate such a person lived and died. Not only that, but often a child of three or four has correctly identified those he claimed were once his family and friends.

"Richard's artistic talent may show he is such a case."

The doctor reached for my mother's hand before continuing.

"With your permission, we would like to investigate. We have discussed applying for a grant from a private organization interested in such studies.

"Of course, Richard would be treated with utmost care and respect. We would not expect either of you to take on added obligations without compensation. If you allow us to proceed, we will request a decent compensation for your participation.

"Our interest rests solely in the advancement of knowledge. Richard will not be subjected to media attention or people seeking to profit from him. Richard's and your involvement could make a substantial contribution to our knowledge of several aspects of human consciousness."

The brain specialist paused, his hands gripping mother's tightly. "It will be long and sometimes tedious work. We may not learn anything. We don't even know what questions to look into. Your willingness to help would be a fine humanitarian gesture."

I felt a wave of incredible joy. A thunderbolt of brilliance filled my being. Briefly, a vision of Samantha's smile eradicated everything from my mind.

"Look, Doctor," said Mother. "Richard is smiling."

THE END